Writing an

A Pencils and What-not Miscellany

This collection Copyright © Pencils and What-not, 2011.

Copyright on individual works remains with their authors.

Published in Great Britain by Pencils and What-not.

For more information see www.pencilsandwhat-not.com

All rights reserved. No part of this publication may be reproduced, stored or introduced into any retrieval system or transmitted in any form, by any means, electronic, mechanical, photocopying, recording, or otherwise, without the prior written permission of Pencils and What-not. Any person who does any unauthorised act in relation to this publication may be liable to criminal prosecution and civil claims for damages.

ISBN: 978-0-9571003-0-5

Printed and bound in Great Britain by Lonsdale Print Solutions Ltd.

Editors: Christina Cummings, Carole Hastings, Gill Johnson, Madeleine Woosnam

Layout: Maria Watson

Cover designer: Kirsty Whittle

Technical advisor: Simon Applebaum

Illustrators: Kay Adamson, Marjorie Andrews, Christina Cummings, Elise Filleul, Maria Watson, Barbara Winnard

Title page photo: Used with permission from Microsoft

This book is dedicated to
our families, friends and Nicky Morris

Contents

Introduction 11
    Hilary Gregory

Winchester 13
    Hilary Gregory

Word Play 14
    Madeleine Woosnam

Pottery and Pansy 17
    Di Reid

In Pursuit of Eavesdropping 21
    Carole Hastings

Mayhew's First Cadaver 25
    Kirsty Whittle

Frank and Ethel 33
    Anne Ponsonby

A Weekend Guest 42
    Angela Ramsell

Rainbow Sherbet 46
    Christina Cummings

Boy Dancer 48
    Claudia Pettifer

Contents

A Villanelle 50
    Gill Johnson

You Should Have Been There 52
    Jenny McRobert

The Lamp Post Swing 54
    Marjorie Andrews

The Magpie 55
    Maria Watson

Amy's Special Day 65
    Peggie Keeley

Roy's Place 70
    Sally Thompson

Lovely Smile 72
    Sonja Eagle

Bitter Lemon 76
    Christina Cummings

The Guy who Spins the Waltzer 78
    Di Reid

The London in Me 86
    Hilary Gregory

Pas de Deux 88
    Jenny McRobert

Contents

Carbuncles and Marigolds 92
    Kirsty Whittle

Travels with Yankee Stellar 95
    Angela Ramsell

The Train 100
    Sally Thompson

When Your Number's Up 102
    Gill Johnson

May – My Best Friend 111
    Marjorie Andrews

On Writing the Village Pantomime 118
    Madeleine Woosnam

Our Last Day in Amazonia 124
    Carole Hastings

Reflections 127
    Sonja Eagle

Pear Season 129
    Christina Cummings

The Tea Party 143
    Anne Ponsonby

Oedipus, Shmoedipus 149
    Jenny McRobert

Contents

Village Competition 151
    Claudia Pettifer

A Not So Vintage Tale 158
    Angela Ramsell

Cooking up some Office Gossip 160
    Carole Hastings

Written in Stone 162
    Hilary Gregory

The River 164
    Madeleine Woosnam

Salut d'Amour 166
    Maria Watson

A Small Man 168
    Jenny McRobert

The Journey 170
    Peggie Keeley

Two Biscuits and a Gas Mask 171
    Marjorie Andrews

Warm Beer and Spam Sandwiches 178
    Anne Ponsonby

Pond on Army Land 182
    Hilary Gregory

Contents

Red Is Not Always For Danger 184
    Peggie Keeley

Jam Jar 185
    Christina Cummings

Total Solar Eclipse 187
    Maria Watson

Flitting on a Friday at the Jubilee Clock 188
    Carole Hastings

Memory 190
    Gill Johnson

Fish Wife 192
    Kirsty Whittle

For the Sake of a Few Dead Roses 193
    Sonja Eagle

April 196
    Di Reid

Diamond Finish 198
    Madeleine Woosnam

Doing the Right Thing 203
    Carole Hastings

Peacock Street 214
    Christina Cummings

Contents

Over the Garden Wall 217
    Di Reid

Suffrage 219
    Marjorie Andrews

Book 501 220
    Maria Watson

The Moon and Our Stars 223
    Sally Thompson

Snow on Christmas Morning 225
    Hilary Gregory

Joshua Frederick Arthur Scott Green 227
    Kirsty Whittle

A Fairly Story 229
    Gill Johnson

Biographies 237

Introduction

In 2010, a group of women set up *Pencils and What-not* in Winchester, to share our passion for writing. We have met once a month since to write, tell stories, read poems, discuss ideas about the craft of writing, chat, laugh, cry and sometimes, to eat cake.

In small buddy groups we cajole, criticise and celebrate each other's endeavours. Supporting each other to write well is as important as producing our own polished pieces. I am happy to say that many of the contributors in this book have enjoyed public success, and we are all proud to have played a part, however small.

This book is a selection of Pencils and What-not's writing on matters great and small and it presents something special about each writer's unique outlook.

Read between the lines to find out more and maybe read some of the work out loud to hear the timbre of the different voices. We hope you will enjoy reading the stories, poems, anecdotes and journal accounts as much as we have enjoyed writing them.

Hilary Gregory
Chair, Pencils and What-not

Winchester

There is a city with Keats's Autumn views,
shops, a butter cross, and a museum of loos,
a hospital that's over 600 years old where
monks give you ale in a Wayfarer's Dole.

There's a working Mill, a theatre called Attic,
a giant bronze statue controlling the traffic,
an annual Hat Fair, lots of places for tea
in what was once the capital, just off the M3.

There's a fake Round Table, burnt cakes in a kitchen
and you can follow ducks along the River Itchen
to an Arbour where ancient roads and Roman walls
once surrounded Anglo Saxon market stalls.

There's a house that was lived in by Jane Austen,
an awesome cathedral that holds her coffin,
a prison, a portcullis, a majestic Westgate
and there - Hyde's the grave of Alfred the Great.

Hilary Gregory

Word Play

Oh stationary stationery sitting in piles
In the stationery cupboard of Douglas and Myles
The mounds of A4, ten envelopes more
And rubbers and rulers for useless young toolers.
And static elastic, just waiting in bands
Like popstars and rockstars in faraway lands.

While out in the office officially sitting
Secretaries file their nails while they're knitting
And secretly yearning and outwardly gurning
As lost loves lose heart and make a new start.
'Hello' I'm 'OK' at the end of the day
'Cosmopolitan' girls. What more can I say?

The boss bosses fussily over her plans
And lines up her minions in cannots and cans
The haves and have-nots, or the company rots
The company she keeps in her bed when she sleeps
Frustrated, castrated for rarely she's sated
And anyway sex is so overrated.

Word Play – Madeleine Woosnam

The Director's directing, the general direction
No time for excuse or rank insurrection.
For the relative styles of Douglas and Myles
Relate to relations of large conurbations.
Like little Jack Horner, he sits in his corner
His career is now over; he's merely the mourner.

And down in Dispatch they're despatching the news
New news in the papers, the popular views.
Now on the top floor in room twenty-four,
A young man in Law hears a knock on the door.
It's the girl from Creative who's come to enquire
If the inquest's inquiry is sure to misfire.

A fly flies in circles and settles on files
In the stationery cupboard of Douglas and Myles.
Essentially sentient sentinel pencils
Leap out of their boxes to dabble with stencils
The bands start their rocking, the noise level's shocking
And paper clips clipping while everything's slipping ...

...and sliding and riding, the A4 is gliding,
The A5 is hiding, the envelopes striding
To get through the window so high over there
And fly away, sky away, never a care
And never no more to be shut for the whiles
In the stationary cupboard of Douglas and Myles.

Madeleine Woosnam

Pottery and Pansy
Di Reid

Pansy's relatives were scattered all over the front and back garden, amongst her pottery mushrooms. They could be seen up to no good in the bushes, pushing wheelbarrows, gazing heavenward, pointed hats at jaunty angles. Looking dopey, distracted, lecherous, and loopy. Peering at balance sheets, knitting, holding baby gnomes, sleeves rolled up ready for work. Three cousins standing on each other's shoulders. Football gnomes, chubby, thin, tall, short, spectacled, shocked, and randy, miserable, happy and smiling gnomes. Hiding behind plant pots, fishing in the pond, and even mooning. In fact the sum total of everyone's relatives. She even had a plaque made for the garden gate, 'Beware of the Gnomes.'

The neighbours hated these naff objects of curiosity, but passers-by loved them. Pansy's husband Ray tolerated them, and escaped to his garden shed. Closing the door he would sink into his old chair and blot the wretched things out of his mind, as yet another one was strategically placed.

The usual plethora of people stood at the bus stop on a Thursday afternoon waiting for the No. 21 bus. Grannies with pull-along shopping baskets, careworn women in drab coloured clothing and lack lustre eyes, young girls wearing skimpy skirts, pierced belly buttons, cleavages to die for, and gangly, spotty teenage boys doing just that.

Pansy stood out from the crowd, alarmingly so. Dressed in layers of loose fitting turquoise, pink and yellow tops, and a long purple skirt. Feet peeping out in bright red and gold trainers. Bangles battered against her capacious tasselled linen bag, and elongated earrings glittering like a thousand stars brushed against her shoulders. She had a sequinned multi-coloured scarf tied round her head like a hair band, ends trailing down her back failing miserably to contain her permed frizzy red hair.

Pansy was off to her pottery and sculpture class at the Institute of Higher Education in Bromley. She loved it, and after the initial introduction and the first term over, she made it quite plain that she wanted to be left alone to sculpt and paint her garden gnomes.

As a child she fell in love with 'Snow White and the Seven Dwarfs.' Bashful, Doc, Dopey, Grumpy, Happy, Sneezy and Sleepy. She didn't care for her own name, and when she complained to her mother Rose, she was told to think herself very lucky as Auntie Lily wanted to call her Petunia.

The No. 21 bus arrived; Pansy found a seat and went back to day-dreaming for the twenty minutes it took to arrive at her stop.

She greeted everyone in class, went to her usual place by the window and opened her bag. She took out a photograph of Auntie Myrtle, and thought that she would sculpt her reading a Mills and Boon book. Pansy loved the feel of the clay in her hands, and glancing at the photograph from time to time she moulded and sculptured it into shape. When she was satisfied with the finished product, she put it on a shelf ready for painting next week. Next to the kiln, fired, and looking splendid, stood Uncle Fred holding his fishing rod.

Class over, Pansy carefully lifted the finished version of Uncle Fred into her bag, and made her way to the bus stop. This was always a worrying time as she held the gnome closely to her, trying to avoid all the pushing and shoving as the bus came into view.

Arriving home she decided it was time for a telephone call.

'Hello Uncle Cyril, would you and Auntie Violet care to come over for tea on Sunday?'

'I'll just see what Vi thinks,' he said, and was back in a minute arranging a time.

Wickedly Pansy would take each of her relatives in turn around the garden, and sit them down next to a gnome looking exactly like them.

'What do you think of my latest little darling Auntie Violet?'

'Very nice dear I'm sure.'

'That one over there looks suspiciously like our Marigold,' said Uncle Cyril.

'Rubbish Cyril, you'll be saying this one looks like me next.'

No-one ever recognises themselves thought Pansy, even Ray couldn't see himself, but they could often recognise their relatives. We never do see ourselves as others see us thought Pansy, even if we are staring at the evidence before our very eyes, and she smiled mischievously to herself.

In Pursuit of Eavesdropping
Carole Hastings

I was getting desperate. Who would have thought it would have been so difficult? As a child I'd wanted to be a spy, so thought this task would be a doddle. But no – time was running out and I was in grave danger of my homework "Be inspired to write after eavesdropping," being pure fabrication.

Stupidly I'd eradicated one eavesdropping opportunity. I'd walked into Winchester from my writing class rather than getting the bus. A quick coffee at Monde proved fruitless, a bit of pointless air-kissing and 'Oh my Gods,' from some soppy schoolgirls – nothing to get your teeth into there.

Usually I'm grumpy if there's too much yakking in the library, but in hope, I hurried along there for the last half hour. The silence was deafening. Perhaps impending exams meant that students were actually studying. I had an 'Oh my God' moment.

The next day I met a friend at the new Westfields Centre in London. I generally hate shopping malls, but Jackie shops, or at least looks, for England, so I felt my homework might be "on a plate" as they say. I settled down on the bus and looked about. The well-heeled were reading the papers. The younger elements were i-podding and head-banging to themselves. The others who managed a few words spoke in a selection of languages unknown to me.

We had a coffee almost immediately and I carried the tray to a table situated next to a table of four people. Jackie must have thought I was mad – the rest of the place was empty. As I took my first sip I discovered that my fellow coffee drinkers were German. I failed my German 'O' level so was foiled again.

The shops were empty too – what an earth is De Beers Diamonds etc. doing in Shepherds Bush? Then I spied a few people in The White Company. A couple of women were admiring the pyjamas. One mentioned the word 'holiday'. Was this it? Could I get some material here? I shuffled over, standing probably a bit too close. I hate people invading my personal space. They clearly felt this too and left swiftly throwing me a weird look. Lunch beckoned. Oh no! The tables in Pizza Express were far too apart to follow any coherent words.

The next day we went to the pub. Again I opted for a table close to a gang of people all of whom were chatting reasonably loudly. As my husband brought the drinks over they all stood up – it was time to have a fag break outside. Momentarily I hated the law. But in no time they all trooped back in, more garrulous than before.

'One, two, one, two,' came the croaking voice over the mic. Yes – it was a local band about to burst our eardrums. I love live music in pubs and the R&B was great. But eavesdropping by lip-reading is just not on.

A day passed and I needed to hop on the bus. This was now my final opportunity. The bus pulled up and yes there were two women who clearly knew each other chatting. They looked like pretty normal middle-aged women, comfortable in each other's company. I might be in for a treat here. Hallelujah! I slunk in behind them and tuned in my ears.

'When's your daughter's baby due then?'

'July 15th. She's going to call her Jade after that Jade Goody who died of cancer.'

'Mmmm.'

Then silence.

What kind of response is "Mmmm?" Did this denote indifference? Bewilderment? Disbelief? This was taking neutrality too far! I was in grave danger of over-stepping the mark and joining in. I didn't even know these women but felt myself becoming angry. It is absolutely awful when anyone dies before their time, especially a young mother. However this act of naming some unsuspecting baby after a foul-mouthed woman who, at best should be pitied but certainly not lauded, seemed like madness. The Max Clifford Roadshow has ensured that Ms Goody will have more than her 15 minutes of fame.

The women left the bus. My anger turned to sadness. I hope the Hampshire Lass has thought again when she saw her own daughter's face staring up at her and gave her a name of beauty, or joy, or even one that she just really likes.

Mayhew's First Cadaver
Kirsty Whittle

This story is inspired by the first line of Roald Dahl's 'The Swan,' published in 1977 by Jonathan Cape.

On his fifteenth birthday, Ollie received just one gift.

A Ruger .22 rifle.

He hadn't always received presents like that.

For his first birthday, for example, although he didn't remember it, he had been given a trolley that he could push along, with a set of 26 lettered bricks that sat inside it and spelt out strange words like *hfkis* and *desnba*, depending on how he placed them. Sometimes his mother, with her round cheeks and her oh-so-warm embrace, would sit with him and rearrange them, and then they would say *cat*. Or *dog*. Or *olie*.

For his ninth birthday, like many nine-year-olds, Ollie got a bike. A Raleigh Velocity, with a speedometer that his Dad had fixed to the handle bars, because he was the sort of Dad who knew what you really wanted when you were a nine-year-old boy.

And for his twelfth birthday Ollie had received a remote control aeroplane that Ollie and his Mum and Dad took over to the fields, because his twelfth birthday fell on a Sunday, and they had all day to do whatever they wanted. Ollie loved the aeroplane. He thought it the very best present he had ever received. Even better than the Raleigh Velocity with the speedometer fixed to the handlebars. But he only loved it for three hours and twenty-four minutes, because at 10.54am on his twelfth birthday, his parents, (who had just climbed over a fence into the adjacent wood to search for the plane which had dropped from the sky due to Ollie's lack of flying hours,) were both shot dead by an angry farmer with .22 rifle, who thought they were poachers.

And that is how Ollie came to live 4,742 miles away in Double Oak, Texas, with Uncle Blake, his father's (much) older brother, who Ollie had hardly heard of, other than the odd Christmas card.

And for his thirteenth and fourteenth birthdays he got nothing at all.

But when he turned fifteen, his Uncle decided it was time the boy had a gun.

*

Ollie started off shooting empty cans lined up on the wall in the back yard. He progressed on to rows of dimes balanced diligently on their sides by his Uncle, who had finally discovered something about the boy he found engaging.

Then Ollie began shooting floating leaves every fall. Hundreds of shantung maple leaves lay in Uncle Blake's yard with perfectly round holes through the centre, each hole .22 inches across, like a carpet of flat, yellow, stigmated hands.

And by the time he was seventeen Ollie was the best junior shot in Denton County, winning 1000 US dollars for beating off the competition.

On his eighteenth birthday Ollie didn't hang out with the boys from Billy Ryan High. He didn't travel with rest of the Denton County Junior Rifle Club to the Texas State finals, which happened, that year, to fall on that very day. And he didn't walk the six hundred and seventeen yards round to the Peterson's house to sweet-talk Mrs P., then creep out back with her daughter to kiss those oh-so-soft-Samantha-Peterson lips.

Instead, five weeks before, Ollie had paid a visit to Oceans'N'Air, Lewisville, and bought himself a return flight to London, England. He booked fourteen nights in a Dorset farmhouse, and applied for a visitor's firearms permit.

And at the precise age of eighteen years, one day, seven hours and thirty-two minutes, Ollie found himself sitting at a kitchen table opposite a Dorset farmer not long out of jail.

Ollie worked his way slowly through a delicious English cheddar ploughman's lunch, with two different types of pickle and four thick slices of home-made granary bread, while his feet rested on his .22 rifle, safely locked up in a gun case under the table.

Ollie thought the English cheddar was the very best cheese he'd tasted in at least six years.

The farmer didn't say much. He sat, and watched his wife fuss around the kitchen. Eventually she brought him a mug of thick tea and placed it on the table in front of him.

The farmer picked it up and a tea-coloured circle was left behind. A tea-coloured *zero,* 7.6 centimetres across. It reminded Ollie of the maple leaves in Uncle Blake's back yard. And it reminded him of the yawning, yearning, crater-sized hole that had been left inside the very centre of himself, exactly six years, one day, three hours and twenty-eight minutes ago. The hole that just kept growing and growing, so much that soon, Ollie thought, there might simply be a huge hole, and no Ollie left at all. *Zero.*

The farmer leaned back in his chair, and eyed the rifle case while he drank.

'No unsupervised shooting,' he said finally. 'Wait until the keeper can take you out.' And he left the kitchen.

*

The next morning, on the first full day of his visit, Ollie walked 7.64 miles around the entire perimeter of the farm: through rapeseed, barley, cattle and woodland.

During the following two days he stayed near the farmhouse, observing the movements of the people on the farm. In the afternoons he spent a little time in his room, cleaning up his rifle.

On the fourth day he waited until he was sure everyone would be clear of the house, then walked down the stairs, out of the door, and made his way directly to the woodland on the north-west edge of the farm, which lay adjacent to public fields. All with his .22 rifle slung over his shoulder.

Ollie searched the woods all day.

He looked through bushes, trees and undergrowth. Whenever he heard a sound he would lay on his belly, sniper-like, and aim the rifle, but no one came.

At exactly twenty-nine minutes past eight Ollie looked up into a 62 foot English oak tree, and saw, in the last of the light, the very thing he'd been looking for, lodged in the branches, midway up.

And he started to climb, with the rifle over his shoulder once more.

When he was high enough Ollie reached up for the faded, weather-battered remains of the remote control aeroplane he'd received for his twelfth birthday. He released it from the arms of the tree which had cradled it for so long, and held it while dusk seeped around him like poisoned gas.

After a while Ollie settled himself into the V between two boughs, and he propped the base of his rifle on a branch just below, so that it pointed up towards the top of the tree. When Ollie looked down, he could barely see a thing now, so he was surprised, when he looked up, at how clearly the moon lit the sky and silhouetted the leaves above him. He considered shooting a few, for old time's sake, and flicked the safety catch off.

But then, abruptly, an overwhelming tiredness engulfed his body. His head felt heavy, and he rested his chin on the end of the barrel.

And Ollie stayed like that for a while, resting, and clutching the dirty, brittle, plastic plane. He thought about Samantha Peterson's soft lips, and recalled the feel of her thighs under his fingers, as smooth as a rifle chamois. Then his mind began to wander. He thought about how many different types of pickle there might be in the world, and about how satisfying it was to see a row of twenty dimes balancing on their sides.   Perhaps he'd try it with twenty British five pence coins. He thought about the bike he used to have when he lived in England, only 2.74 miles away from this very spot, as it happened. There had been a speedometer on the handlebars, he remembered.

Occasionally a voice crept into his thoughts. 'Boy?' it said, faintly.   'Boy? Are you out here? Can you hear me?' Ollie thought vaguely that it might be Uncle Blake, but what was he doing so far from Double Oak? And why was he speaking with an English accent?

He ignored it.

Ollie didn't know how long he stayed in the tree. It could have been minutes, or hours.   It could have been weeks. Time didn't seem to matter too much now.

At some point his thoughts started to become a little fuzzy. More *feels,* really, than *thoughts*. He felt an embrace, oh-so-warm.   And soft, round cheeks against his.   A happiness flooded into his body as unstoppable as that induced by Samantha Peterson's kisses (perhaps even *more* unstoppable.) And, unfathomably, right at the end, Ollie's mind simply formed two strange words: *hfkis* and *desnba*.

Then, suddenly, nothing. Zero.

*

Two days, fourteen hours and twenty-nine minutes later, Inspector Stephen Hatcher looked up into the tree, and then back down at the cadaver at his feet. He had been an inspector for only fifteen days, but he fancied he knew a close range .22 exit wound when he saw one, especially when a .22 rifle lay not three feet away from the victim.

A messy, ragged, blood-caked hole, 1.23 inches across, gaped at him from the side of Ollie's head.

'Suicide, Sir?'

Inspector Stephen Hatcher counted to five. It didn't do to reply to these rookies too quick – he needed to create an air of authority now that he was an inspector.

'Looks like it, Mayhew, but we can't be certain. Farmer up here's got a history of this sort of thing, as I'm sure you'll remember.'

Or perhaps not, he thought, as the ridiculously youthful WPC Mayhew looked over at him blankly. Probably still in pigtails six years ago. *Jesus.*

'Come on, Mayhew, we need an I.D. on this kid. And where are those forensic nerds? Has no one called the Coroner's yet?'

Frank and Ethel

Anne Ponsonby

Ethel looked again at the advertisement in the newspaper. "Situation vacant for gentlewoman. Must have good speaking voice and be prepared to travel."

She was very tempted to send an answer to the box number provided. What was stopping her? She had just had her birthday, having been born towards the end of Queen Victoria's reign. What had she achieved in her life so far?

Her father had died when she was twelve years old, leaving her mother with so little money that the whole family had to live with an uncle who reluctantly offered them a roof over their heads. He expected quite a lot in return. She was fond of her mother but her twin sisters, Laura and Margaret, were so close to each other that there was no room for her opinions or ideas. Her brother was working in a bank and rarely came home. She saw a life ahead of her with nothing to look forward to.

Women were still expected to marry young, bear many children, look after their husbands and any elderly relatives "until death did them part." It was now 1911 and horizons were beginning to widen. The suffragette movement was just beginning.

Ethel had secret dreams of travelling to distant lands, meeting someone to marry, or failing that to become a person in her own right. Her organisational skills were very useful, but she had no chance to develop them living in a small village near Cambridge.

'Ethel' her mother called from the kitchen, 'I need several things from the village, could you please get them for me?'

She set off with the list, a shopping basket and enough money but no more. It started to rain and before long her skirt was covered in mud, her shoes were damp and her long, chestnut coloured hair was dripping. Of course she had forgotten her battered umbrella. On her return she dumped the basket in the kitchen, went to change her clothes and took another look at the advertisement.

Over a cup of tea she made a decision.

'Mother', I want to go to London and stay with Cousin Elizabeth, just for a few days.'

'London?' her mother looked bewildered. 'Why London? And you don't even like Cousin Elizabeth. How are you going to pay the fare?'

'Please, could you lend me the money? I really want to go and I promise to pay it back – Mrs Jones wants me to make some curtains for her bedroom and she'll pay me well because my sewing is so good.'

Her mother sipped her tea and remained silent for a few minutes. Ethel had always been a loving and dutiful daughter but her chestnut hair went with a fiery temper. Sometimes it exploded – only occasionally - but it looked as if it might be simmering at the moment.

Reluctantly she gave her permission. No sooner had she done so, Ethel wrote to her cousin, found a battered bag in the loft and started planning her journey.

London was a mystery. She had never been further than Norwich a few miles away. She was excited, nervous and anxious all at the same time. Her letter to Elizabeth was written and posted.

The answer came by return of post. "Yes," wrote Elizabeth, "I can give you a bed for a couple of nights but I cannot imagine why you want to come to London? You always told me you hated big cities and never wanted to leave the country. I suppose you have your reasons. Let me know what time to expect you. I would be pleased if you would bring me some fresh farm eggs and a jar of honey."

Ethel wrapped the eggs carefully in her suitcase and prayed they would not break. The train journey was long and there were several delays. Finally arriving in London, she took a hansom cab to Edgware Road where Elizabeth lived.

The welcome was lukewarm. Her cousin was a serious, humourless spinster. She had been a teacher in her younger days and still spoke as if she was in front of a blackboard. Her greying hair was put up in a formidable looking bun.

Having greeted Ethel, she took the eggs and honey saying, 'I hope these eggs are really fresh? And I would have preferred thick honey, not this runny kind.'

After unpacking her few belongings, Elizabeth told her to come through into the bleak little kitchen where she had prepared a very simple supper.

'So, why on earth have you come to London?'

'Well, I've got an interview with an agency and I hope there may be a vacancy with a family as a companion or a governess. Please try and understand – I must get away from home and see something of the world.'

A long discussion followed. Arguments flew back and forth. Tempers started to fray and Ethel went to bed feeling even more anxious, having been told she was an undutiful daughter and should know better.

The next morning she dressed with care and put on her best long skirt and a high necked blouse, both made by herself and very becoming. She was tall with a slender figure, a long neck, and hazel eyes. Her thick hair was her pride and joy. She spent time coiling it on top of her head. A pretty straw hat completed her outfit and she set off in plenty of time.

A brother and sister, Agatha and Edward Fletcher, had started the agency some years before. It had been successful due to the care and attention paid by the owners. It was unusual for a woman to work at all, but Agatha was a skillful interviewer and seemed to have a sixth sense when placing the right person in the right position.

She wanted to find someone exceptional for this position.

Edward Fletcher announced the arrival of Miss Ethel Bates and left his sister with her.

First impressions were positive. Agatha noticed the care and attention to Ethel's appearance. Her shoes were polished, her skirt and blouse well ironed, her hair clean and tidy, her posture upright and she seemed composed and confident.

A detailed discussion about Ethel and her general health, education and family took about ten minutes. Agatha paused. So far, she was impressed. She asked,

'Miss Bates, I haven't yet told you anything about the

position available. It is mainly to work as a governess with four children. These children are very well educated and already speak good English, as well as German, French and Italian. You would live as part of the family in a city but also out in the country. First of all, are you prepared to travel and live in a foreign country?'

'Oh yes, I really do want to see something of the world, that's why I applied in the first place.'

'I'll tell you,' she paused, 'The country is Russia, and the city is St Petersburg.'

Ethel drew a deep breath and waited.

'Secondly, and most importantly the Head of the Household is Count Pahlen and he is a Lord in Waiting to the Tsar of Russia.'

Ethel took another deep breath.

Agatha paused once more. 'Do you feel able to consider this position?'

Without a moment's hesitation, Ethel replied 'Yes, I am prepared to go to Russia and would like to accept the position.'

Many miles away, across the Atlantic Ocean, in Ottawa the capital of Canada, Frank Maynard was having a lengthy discussion with his father. Frank was also 29 years old and had recently graduated as an officer from the Royal Military College, in Kingston, Ontario.

He had four brothers and a sister. The family was close but recently there had been an upsetting episode in the form of a beautiful, young French Canadian lady with whom Frank had been in love. There was strong disapproval from his parents, mainly due to the fact that Marie Louise was a Roman Catholic. The Maynards were Presbyterian with Scottish and Northern Ireland ancestry.

The discussion continued. Frank explained to his father that he wanted to go to Europe, learn another language and thus increase his pay. He had chosen Russian and had been accepted as a student in Moscow for one year. He had agreed to break off his relationship with Marie Louise. In return he wanted his parent's encouragement to go overseas.

His father took time to give his opinion. After a lengthy pause he said,

'I think you should go. Your education is not complete until you have experienced living in another country and Russia is a good choice. The Tsar is an autocratic ruler and it looks as if the people are becoming restless. Therefore the sooner you go and learn the language, the better for your future career.'

Frank was relieved. His love for his family was genuine but he needed to stretch his wings and his mind. Preparations were quickly made and before long he found himself in London, waiting for the day he would sail for St. Petersburg.

Ethel had also been busy. She was nervous at the thought of going to an unknown country and to live with a family with such high connections. She had made herself some new clothes including a winter coat in olive green, trimmed with fur. She also wore a hat she had re-furbished with more fur. Her arrival at Tilbury dock was noticed by Frank who watched her walk up the gangway.

He turned to his friend. 'Arthur', he said 'Do you see that young lady with the chestnut hair?'

'Yes,' replied Arthur. 'What about her?'

'She is the woman I am going to marry.'

*

Frank and Ethel were my parents. Their courtship on board ship was brief. They were separated for a year, he in Moscow, she in St Petersburg, but wrote to each other every day. I still have my father's romantic letters which I have kept for many years. For some reason her letters to Frank have disappeared but no doubt were equally romantic.

They were re-united a year later and married in 1914 the year that the First World War broke out. They were separated for some time as my father was fighting, first in Mesopotamia (which is now Iraq) and later, in France. He received the MC for his bravery and sustained a wound which left a bullet in his head. As children we loved feeling the little lump which could have killed him.

My twin sisters, Diana and Patricia, were born in 1915. After the War, my father decided to transfer to the Indian Army which would increase his pay. I was born in Peshawar, Pakistan, and my mother became a true soldier's wife moving every two or three years until my father's retirement in 1936.

The story of their courtship has become part of the family history, told and re-told. My sisters each had six children, which together with my three, formed a numerous clan. On one occasion when we gathered nearly all the family together, we numbered well over one hundred people with an age range from eighty down to three months.

How did this story begin? An advertisement in a newspaper? A young woman with a desire to make something of herself? A young man who also wanted to widen his horizons and stretch his brain? Call it Fate or Providence. You choose.

A Weekend Guest
Angela Ramsell

He arrived on Friday, with his own food, medication and bed. He is portly, deaf as a post, has arthritic limbs and is named Hervey (pronounced Harvey). He is a border collie, litter mate of my dog Lucy but looks much older than her.

Friday was reasonably uneventful as far as I was concerned. Lucy, however, obviously didn't agree as he insisted on sleeping on her bed and when he wasn't sleeping would try to mount her, in spite of the fact that he was castrated at six months, he just can't resist trying to prove he's still game.

Bedtime arrived. From past experience I knew that if I shut him downstairs in the study, he would bark intermittently all night, so I decided to let him sleep on the landing outside my bedroom door. I put Lucy's bed up there and shut the door quickly before he invaded my territory. It was late so I settled down to sleep. When I heard Hervey tap-dancing in the bathroom, I told myself he'll settle down soon. When he threw himself against the bedroom door nearly ripping it off its hinges, I told myself he'll settle down soon. When he thudded up and down the stairs twice, I told myself he'll settle down soon. Eventually all went quiet and I drifted off to sleep.

'Yip, yap, yip, yap.' My eyes shot open, what was that?

'Yip, yap, yip, yap.' Oh no, it was Hervey. I peered at the time on my digital clock. 1.45. I lay there; eyes open wide in the dark. He'd gone quiet. I peered at the clock again. 1.50. I closed my eyes and started to relax. Soon I was drifting off.

'Yip, yap, yip, yap.' My eyes shot open again and for the third time I peered at the clock, 2.30. Best get up and let him out in the garden.

Downstairs and into the kitchen we went. He headed for the water bowl not the back door. I went over to get him by the collar, no point calling a deaf dog. He very kindly dribbled water all over my bare feet, just to make sure I was fully awake. I took him over to the back door and let him out. He immediately disappeared into the shadows of the trees. I stood there straining my eyes looking for his white patches. After about five minutes he reappeared and stood about eight feet away from me. I tried signalling that he should come in. No response. Eventually I had to trail over the damp grass to grab his collar to get him in. Off up to bed again. Settling down was a bit quicker this time. He missed out the bathroom tap dance and simply threw himself the bedroom door and had a good scratch, his leg banging against the door rhythmically like a bass drum. Finally, quiet. Off to sleep again.

'Yip, yap, yip, yap. Yip, yap, yip, yap.' I could feel an "incredible hulk" moment coming on. My muscles started to bulge and I could swear I was turning green and growing hair on my chest. I visualised my hands encircling his neck and squeezing tightly. I took some deep breaths and tried to relax. I looked at the clock, 3.30. I opened my bedside table drawer and fumbled about eventually getting hold of some ear plugs I had in there. I stuffed them in my ears and turned over. It took me ages to get back to sleep. Not so Hervey. Even with my ear plugs in I could hear him snoring loudly outside my door. Sleep came and I slept until 6.30 when I heard the inevitable 'Yip, yap, yip, yap.' Time to get up.

Later on Saturday, I had to go out shopping. I shut Lucy in the study and looked around for Hervey. He was sleeping peacefully in a patch of sun by the back door. Well, he had had a bad night. I took pity on him. I thought he can't do any harm sleeping there in the kitchen and if I leave the door open he'll have the run of the hall as well. Big mistake. When I got home, this decrepit, arthritis-ridden old dog had somehow managed to stand on his weak back legs, pull the newly filled dog treat container onto the floor, smashing it in the process, and eaten all the dog treats it had contained.

Yes, you've guessed, another night of 'Yip, yap, yip, yap.' With Hervey and me trudging up and down stairs and into the garden whilst he unloaded his ill-gotten gains.

Sunday night both Hervey and I slept like babies and tonight he'll be sleeping in his own house. Yippee or should I say 'Yippee, yappee, yippee, yappee.'

Rainbow Sherbet

Christina Cummings

Brushing winter from the sleeves of my coat, I sense I'm being watched and look up to find enquiring eyes and tear-stained cheeks beholding me.

A little boy, no more than three years old, blinks away his mother's harsh words. He's facing backwards on the seat in front, kneeling up as though in prayer.

'Turn around,' his mother drawls. The boy looks at me, hesitates, and wags a brightly stained fingertip before my nose.

'I told you to sit down!' Tired hands prise him, turn him, press him into the seat.

This city bus accelerates, sucked by the flow, absorbed by smog-choked streets. A moment passes, I hear the rustle of a paper bag and then, slow as he can, he steals a last glance. Beneath a stripy bobble hat, barely peeking, he gestures towards the grimy windowpane. Tiny damp fingertips, caked with coloured sherbet crystals seem to be saying, 'Look!'

Outside, snowflakes, big as leaves, tumble from the greyness. They cartwheel and piggyback, melt into the tarmac. Pressing his tiny nose flat against the glass, to get a better view, I hear a happy gurgle escape from his lips.

'Get up!' the boy's mother says, and feeding his sticky hands into stale mittens, pulls him along the aisle. She holds him up by the armpits, to ding the bell.

'It's our stop,' she whispers into his warm neck. Tucking the paper bag deep into the secret pocket of her shopping bag, she sets him down and together they sway and falter until the bus stands still. I watch them as they walk away, hand in hand along the tree-lined street, like two tiny figures now, in a giant snow-globe. The boy does not look back. Mesmerised by a new world of white promise, he disappears into the flurry, as the bus pulls away into the steady traffic.

Boy Dancer
Claudia Pettifer

Wanted: Boy Dancers Abu Dhabi - Experience Not Essential

Obviously I hadn't actually *bought* the magazine this ad appeared in. Believe me, sixteen-year-old boys from Oldham wouldn't be seen dead buying anything that didn't have a car or a large pair of tits on the front, but after sitting for thirty-seven minutes in the waiting room of the doctor's surgery, staring at the steady flow of women with sniffling toddlers and shuffling old people coughing their guts up, I was desperate. Faced with a choice of *Family Circle, Practical Caravaner* or *Star!* I picked up the latter wondering if it had a local gig guide.

I'd left school that summer with a GCSE in Art and socially crippling case of acne (hence the trip to the docs). Needless to say Mum and Dad were "disappointed" but it wasn't my fault. Bloody Thatcher (for a large part of my childhood I thought *Bloody* was her Christian name) and a crap inner city school were to blame in my opinion. Anyway the chances of getting a job round there were infinitesimal even *with* GCSEs and interpersonal skills. Mum said I had the social ability of a gnat. I didn't even know what she meant. And in any case, wasn't it her job to train me?

The advert caught my attention straight off and my imagination started to rev up. Abu Dhabi? Isn't that sunny and full of rich people? Images of beaches and beautiful blond women in bikinis popped into my head (they needed little encouragement). No experience necessary? This ad had my name written all over it.

'EDMUND JACKSON.' I was jolted back to reality, and before the receptionist had even finished calling my name I cried out, 'ED! IT'S ED!' - just a little too loudly. But I still looked round to check no one had heard my real name. If word got out, life wouldn't be worth living. Fortunately all around me were either deaf or gaga.

I tore out the ad, shoved it in my pocket and, fantasising there was a new miracle cure for spots, headed into the doc's room.

Note: The quote from a magazine advertisement which opens this piece of writing is a 'borrowed line' from Richard E Grant's With Nails: The Film Diaries of Richard E Grant, published by Picador, May 1996.

A Villanelle

I long to live life in the sun,
For gentle rays to caress my soul,
Where warmth tells weariness be gone.

I yearn for days of carefree fun,
Al fresco suppers are my goal,
I long to live life in the sun.

I crave flowers of yellow and crimson,
Fragrant grasses in which to roll,
Where warmth tells weariness be gone.

I pine for the satin summer season,
Splashing in a honeyed water hole.
I long to live life in the sun.

I hanker for the daylight golden,
Meandering meadows where I can stroll,
Where warmth tells weariness be gone.

A Villanelle – Gill Johnson

I do not care when rains dampen,

And shivers and illness take their toll.

I long to live life in the sun,

Where warmth tells weariness be gone.

Gill Johnson

Note: A villanelle is a structured poem with Line 1 as the refrain 1 a, Line 2 b, Line 3 refrain 2 a, Line 4 a, Line 5 b, Line 6 refrain 1 a, Line 7 a, Line 8 b, Line 9 refrain 2 a, Line 10 a, Line 11 b, Line12, refrain 1 a, Line 13 a, Line 14 b, Line 15 refrain 2 a, Line 16 a, Line 17 b, Line 18, refrain 1 a, Line 19 refrain 2 a..

You Should Have Been There
(Song)

Bob Dylan topped the bill
And I was on the pill
That Woodstock summer
I got off with the drummer
Tousled hair and jangling beads
You should have been there
Oh yeah, you should have been there

They started the space race
For the top place
The U.S. and Russia fight
All in black and white
One small step for man
One giant leap for mankind
You should have been there
Oh yeah, you should have been there

You Should Have Been There - Jenny McRobert

The Beatles 'Love Me Do'
A sound completely new
An overnight sensation
Flamed across the nation
Girls screamed, and fainted
While Andy Warhol painted
Marilyn and tins of soup
You should have been there
Oh yeah, you should have been there

You think you're really cool
But I remember when you used to drool
You're still just a kid
But I'm not just your Mum
Inside I'm the young girl
With the boy and his drum
Still tasting that first kiss
You should have been there
Oh yeah, you should have been there

Jenny McRobert

The Lamp Post Swing

It stood at our door in the street
where we lived

Ropes through the brackets
where the gas mantle hid

It's colour grey and made of
strong iron

There'd be shouts from the kids –
'We're flying, we're flying'

You'd hear 'It is my turn.' Such a terrible din
If I can't have my go I will take my rope in

It was brilliant, exciting, a fabulous treat
The swing on the lamp post that stood in our street

Marjorie Andrews

The Magpie
Maria Watson

On Saturday night Dave and Eddie strolled into the bar, checking out the talent on the way. They took their drinks over to see what Frank had knocked off that week. 'Genuine gold sovereigns, on 18 carat gold chains, only twenty quid!' he called out. Eddie picked up one of the coins and bit it.

'Well, that definitely isn't chocolate. I bet it isn't real gold, either,' he concluded.

Dave looked down at his own white "Fred Perry" tennis shirt, bought from Frank the week before. He wasn't going to waste any more of his hard-earned cash on ersatz finery. He caught Eddie's eye and they walked across to their favourite table, facing the door. Soon, a pair of girls tottered in and nudged each other when they spied Dave's striking black hair, pale face and piercing blue eyes. They started giggling when he smiled at them and stood up so that they could appreciate his six foot frame, broad shoulders and toned glutes squeezed into his fitted jeans. Eddie moved in for the kill.

'Hello ladies. Haven't we seen you somewhere before? You aren't presenters on "Good Morning Essex", by any chance?'

Soon they were sitting at the table sipping Cinzano and lemonade. Dave reached over to the prettiest girl and gently touched the silver turtle dove on her wrist. She told him her Nan had given it to her for her eighteenth birthday, and happily chatted away, recounting the story of each charm on her bracelet. Then he shrugged on his black Harrington jacket and led them off to work their way through the clubs and bars in the High Street.

*

On Sunday morning, Dave awoke with a thumping headache, a mouth like the inside of a leather glove and no recollection of how he'd got home. Mum called up to him,

'I'm off to church now. Put the chicken in the oven. Bye!'

He recalled the last time he'd been in church. Dave and Eddie had belonged to a trio of acolytes who assisted the Rector. The third boy, Patrick, was articulate and well-spoken, but Dave had a stammer and the Rector had never trusted Eddie after the incident with the incense burner. Patrick always read the prayers whilst Dave and Eddie cleaned the altar and held the candles. The Rector would praise Patrick for his clear diction and sensitive expression, then give Dave and Eddie a curt "thank you." The partiality infuriated them, so one Sunday, Eddie rugby tackled Patrick as he crossed the churchyard to Communion, removed his trousers and handed them to Dave, who tossed them up onto the war memorial. Patrick scuttled into the vestry and put his cassock and surplice on before the first member of the congregation arrived to claim the front pew. If she had noticed his bony white shins protruding as he stood at the lectern reading the collect, she had been too polite to mention it. Later, Patrick retrieved his trousers and Dave and Eddie ran home thinking that they had got away with it.

Patrick knew that revenge was a dish best served cold. He persuaded the other boys in their class to send Eddie and Dave "to Coventry." This didn't bother Eddie; he was so garrulous that he could make up both sides of a conversation. He soon had the others laughing so much that they cracked and started talking to him again. Poor Dave was different. Self-conscious about his stammer, he barely spoke at the best of times and being pointedly ignored by the others tipped him over the edge into silence. As the mute days rolled into weeks, teachers began to notice and eventually made arrangements for him to see a speech therapist. This might well have fixed the problem. However, he was fascinated by the "St. Christopher" pendant which danced down the speech therapist's cleavage when she got excited, and he found that refusing to speak was a sure way of exciting her.

He roused himself from this reverie and shoved the chicken in the oven. He was dressed and peeling the potatoes when Mum got back from the service, bursting with news and gossip.

'Your friend, Patrick, is coming back to be our new curate!' she announced.

Dave vigorously sliced down through a cabbage head as he tried to think of a way of avoiding him. For ten years, Mum had persisted in updating Dave on "Golden Boy's" outstanding academic progress, the discovery of his vocation whilst at Cambridge, and the inspiration he had received at theological college. Even when Patrick's Mum died and his Dad moved away, there was no let up. Patrick's Auntie kept Mum informed and Dave was treated to a blow by blow account of his good deeds as a deacon in Stepney.

*

Monday morning arrived all too soon and Dave had to rise early for work. There was no sense in wearing his mod revival gear for this, so he slid into tatty cords, holey sweater and Doc Martens. At the depot he added waterproof trousers and a fluorescent jacket and then got into the street sweeper parked in the yard. It was his turn to drive it round the gutters, spinning the pair of brushes at the front and sucking the debris up. Dave usually preferred doing the manual work, spiking up the litter in the park or hosing the dog shit off the pavements, because it gave him the chance to spot the little treasures that he pocketed as a perk of the job. Today though, he was relieved to be hidden in the cab.

Dave was sweeping the leaves out of the gutter when he felt the brushes strike something heavy. Gingerly probing through the pile of debris, his fingertips felt a large ring, big enough to slip his hand through. He grasped it, pulled upwards and out came a bunch of heavy antique keys. As he turned the keys in his hand, he noticed that the metal shaft of one of them had been given a waist by being repeatedly twisted through a loose lock. He thought he had seen something like it before.

Dave took the key to the church and tested it in the iron lock of the porch grill. Sure enough, the heavy gate swung open. He entered; sniffing the mixture of damp, dust and flowers, and the musty scent brought back childhood memories to him. They weren't all bad. He and Patrick and

Eddie had shared some laughs together jumping up and down on the grass clippings piled up in the corner of the churchyard. They had found wild garlic growing there and dared each other to eat it, then horrified each other by speculating that it had grown out of the ashes scattered on holy ground after cremations. He jumped out of his skin when a hand touched his shoulder and someone said,

'Hello Dave. It's good to see you after so long.'

Spinning round, he saw Patrick, smiling at him. He handed him the keys and tried to walk past, but Patrick was blocking his exit through the grill.

'Thanks very much for bringing these back. I must have dropped them after choir practice last night and I've been hunting for them since I got up this morning.'

Dave nodded and tried to edge past. Patrick stood still and said,

'I've been hoping to catch up with you again. Have you got time to come round for a drink this evening? I'm staying with Auntie, as usual.' Dave nodded and slunk past.

'About 8 o'clock then?' Patrick called after him.

*

Dave kept the appointment, prompted perhaps by the memories brought back at the church, or driven by curiosity to find how "Golden Boy" had really turned out.

'Come in Dave. Thanks very much again for returning those keys. We'd have had to break in through the vestry for Matins if you hadn't. Come through to the kitchen. I've got some cans of Stella in the fridge.'

Dave wasn't keen on lager, but couldn't say no. He wished he'd brought Eddie along to speak for him. He found himself sitting opposite Patrick in a threadbare armchair with a tinnie in his hand. Patrick looked for inspiration to continue their one-sided conversation, and noticed Dave's two-toned patent brogues.

'I've just borrowed "Quadrophenia" from the record library. Shall I put it on?' Dave's face lit up and so he dusted the first LP and put it on the turntable. The two men listened in companionable silence and then Dave stood, indicating that he was ready to go home. Patrick got up to show him out and asked,

'Gonna be one of the faces at my ordination?'

That was the last thing Dave was expecting him to say and he nodded his acceptance in surprise.

'I'd like to ask the Bishop if he'd let you read the Lord's Prayer for us.'

Dave looked very concerned and Patrick reassured him,

'Everyone knows the words. You just say "Our Father" to get them going.'

Patrick wrote down the date and the time of the service on a slip of paper for Dave and said that he would reserve seats at the cathedral for him and his Mum.

'Do you think Eddie would like to come, too?' he asked.

Dave, still in shock at the prospect of reading a prayer at the cathedral, shook his head and fled.

*

Mum was overjoyed when they took their seats near the front. She nudged Dave to take off his trilby, smoothed down her skirt and looked round as the clergy processed up the aisle. Priests and deacons wearing black stoles over white cassocks came first. Good, she thought. Dave won't stand out too much in his black suit and skinny tie. The Bishop followed, resplendent in his cope and mitre. When he reached the chancel steps, he turned to greet the people and started to lead the long service. Eventually Patrick's turn came to be presented and she nudged the dignitary who was sitting on her left.

'He's my son's friend, you know,' she whispered.

Dave, sitting on the other side, turned his face away and hoped the gentleman would not look round. He had been staring at the floor throughout the proceedings, and was acutely aware of the sweat prickling his hair and running down the inside of his arms. Should he take his jacket off? No, everyone would see the white shirt plastered to his skin. Now Mum's sharp right elbow was jabbing him in the ribs.

'The Bishop's invited you to read the prayer. Up you go.'

Dave walked up the aisle, clutching his order of service in trembling hands and still not daring to raise his head. He took care not to trip up the steps and then crossed over to the eagle lectern. He placed the pamphlet on top of the bible, bent the microphone up towards his mouth, and took a deep breath. Nothing came out. He looked down, re-read the familiar words and tried again.

'Our Father,' he whispered.

Someone in the organ loft tweaked up the amplifier on the sound system.

'Which art in heaven,' he croaked.

'Hallowed be thy name,' murmured the congregation. Dave looked up and saw nine hundred, maybe a thousand people, whispering the prayer together with him.

'Thy kingdom come,' he said. He couldn't hear his own voice amongst the others now and he found it helped.

'Thy will be done, on earth as it is in heaven. Give us this day our daily bread.' The words echoed round the pillars of the nave, just as they had done every day for centuries.

'And forgive us our trespasses.' Good grief, that would have tied his tongue in knots before.

'As we forgive those who trespass against us.' He thought he saw Patrick nod. Dave was enjoying himself now and he spoke clearly and loudly until, punching the air in jubilation, he reached the final line,

'For ever and ever, Amen.'

Amy's Special Day
Peggie Keeley

Having worked extra hours, it was good to think she would have time off for that special day. The alarm sounded at 6:30a.m. – plenty of time to have a shower, breakfast and a leisurely hour to pick out her outfit. Less than an hour later she was ready. The town was quite busy – market stalls being loaded with their respective wares; lots of bunting up in the shop windows. Everyone looked so happy, greeting friends and strangers alike.

'Good morning.'

'What's the weather going to be? The reports said possible showers, but they are often wrong.'

'Ah well.' She hoped for the best. Whatever happened she was going to enjoy herself.

Reaching the station, she found that the London train was already in; fortunately she found a seat and relaxed, thinking about the day ahead. Some of the passengers had obviously had an early start and were eating and drinking from their picnic boxes. The children munching crisps and jumping up and down excitedly.

'Tommy, sit down, you're making a mess, don't spill that drink down your clean top – Sharon, stop teasing Jason, it will only end in tears.' It reminded her of Joyce Grenfell and she had to smile, while avoiding the sticky fingers.

Reaching Waterloo, she joined the throng of people pushing towards the barriers. She decided to stop and have a quick coffee and a snack before starting the next phase of her day out.

Finding her bearings, Amy made her way across London. There was such an air of excitement in the air; people were stretching their legs after spending the last few nights camping; lots of laughter and good hearted banter – this was the day. The day they had all been looking forward to – the Royal Wedding Day. There were Union flags everywhere, red white and blue colours in abundance and that lovely feeling of camaraderie which comes in moments of expectation. As she walked along, she could hear so many different accents, broad American, excitable Italian, lots of lilting Welsh, many Japanese with their expensive cameras. There were families having fun with their children, the little ones waving their flags; so much to look at. She rarely saw a policeman in her home town, and there seemed to be hundreds, all being friendly and helpful.

Amy's Special Day – Peggie Keeley

As the time went on, the excitement grew; you could feel it in the air. Would she be able to get a good view? It would be lovely to find a place where she could see the guests.

She made for the Mall hoping that someone would help her find a place near the front of people grouped together, tall, short, large and small in all kinds of outfits, some quite outlandish, others very regal – crowns, tiaras, funny hats – a vast spread of red, white and blue. Amy had a lump in her throat – it was all so incredibly moving – this outburst of patriotism. Now she could hear the bands, the sounds of horses, bells ringing: who was in that car? It was Princess Anne, wasn't it, oh and surely that was Beatrice and Eugenie, now that definitely is the Queen and the Duke of Edinburgh. Her Majesty was looking lovely in a beautiful yellow outfit. The cheering was deafening, but nobody cared, they were all here to join in the celebrations.

While the service was taking place, some of which she could hear on the various speakers and as it came to an end, there was the expectation of the pageantry to come. She chatted with the people around her, discussing what was happening and how soon they would see the people coming back from Westminster Abbey. They could see all the soldiers and airmen lining the route and suddenly there were mounted policemen on their lovely horses and there, oh yes.

'Look it's Prince William and his bride.' They look so happy, waving to the crowds, more horses, now there is Prince Harry with some of the bridesmaids, followed by Philippa Middleton with the little bridesmaids – they look so sweet. Now she could see the grey horses pulling the carriage with the Queen and Prince Philip – more horses and now she could see Prince Charles with Camilla and the Middleton family. By now a lot of the crowd were beginning to collect their belongings and move along to Buckingham Palace, so she went along with them. Still cheering and singing with happiness – she had never seen or heard anything quite like it, and the best feeling was she was part of it all. A young woman with a not very demanding job, today everything felt quite different – she felt she could do anything. When she was back on her home ground, she would think about trying harder to achieve her goal.

As the crowd moved nearer to the Palace, the excitement was greater than ever, the balcony doors were opening and an enormous cheer went up. The Prince and his lovely Bride emerged and accompanied by their families, the best man, Prince Harry resplendent in his uniform with the bridesmaids. What a wonderful picture. The crowd were calling 'Kiss, kiss, kiss,' and, looking a little bashful Prince William obliged. The crowd cheered even louder, so they had an even longer kiss. What bliss.

Following that, a fly past – old planes and new – even a Sea King helicopter.

Now the walk back – it seemed miles, but with so much happiness all around, Amy was back into London en route for the Railway station and the journey home. Luckily, finding a seat, she sat back and went through all she had heard and seen this special day. From the station she walked back to her modest home, made a cup of tea – a little snack – turned on the television and watched the whole day's events in glorious Technicolor. Admiring the outfits of the guests in the Abbey, singing along with the hymns, and enjoying the last moments of her special day out. Tomorrow she would make plans to achieve her goals. So much to look forward to and lovely memories to enjoy. Perhaps there would be a 'special day' especially for her.

Roy's Place

It stands surveying all around
that wind and weather-torn tree
Its hold is steadfast in the ground
A place to set him free

He loved this place, its reach, its peace
over to the Island, up to the Downs
Its majesty beholds everything
for miles and miles abound

And so he took us there one day
hand in hand, in hand to tell
us precisely where to release
him from his beloved land

We come back now and then
to walk, to talk, to be
It holds a special resonance
for him, for her, for me

Roy's Place – Sally Thompson

The scenes from here speak volumes
each have a story to tell from
Navy reaches to farmers breaches
upon the fields they plough

And yet a quiet stillness
consumes the air aloud
as we look and remember him
the days, the man, so proud

He was so full of life and love
gregarious to the end
this place, his place, reminds
us that life is in our hands

Roy's place, our place, your place and mine
from this hill fort we can see Man's
seeming insignificance, yet Roy
you left a space for us to be.

Sally Thompson

Lovely Smile
Sonja Eagle

Sue glanced over at Celia and wondered yet again why she didn't join in any of the social events at the Sunset Nursing Home. She had, after all, been good friends with Celia since she joined the staff there five years ago. Celia was the first friendly face to whom she had been introduced. She remembered to this day her first duty where she had felt totally bewildered when Old Mr. Jenkins had shouted at her and accused her of stealing his jumper. Celia had appeared immediately and helped her ameliorate the situation, soothing Mr. Jenkins and calming her down and she had given them both the benefit of her wonderful all-encompassing smile. All the residents loved Celia's bright friendly face and her in-depth concern over the minutia of their illnesses and their personal lives. She was always there with a tissue or a word of comfort and cared really deeply about the residents.

'Celia are you sure you won't make that drink tonight after this shift?'

'No, sorry Sue, really got to get home.'

'Oh okay Hun, just wondered if I could persuade you for once.'

Sue got back to folding the sheets in an orderly pile and putting them away in the cupboard.   She enjoyed her job at the nursing home. It was a friendly place, light and airy and most of the residents were quite content and happy. Her mind wandered back to some of the other homes she had worked at, where the staff and residents were miserable and often deeply distressed and unhappy. No doubt about it she thought, it was Celia who brought happiness and well-being to this home. It was Celia who insisted on fresh flowers and clean, bright curtains and new games in the common room. It was Celia who also ensured that regular entertainment was provided at least once a week and none of that sitting round with someone banging out old tunes on the piano. No, they had talks, interesting talks about local history and world events. It all helped keep the residents interested and alert. No doubt about it, it was the best place she had ever worked, and she was grateful to Celia for being such a brilliant Matron. The only thing she had ever known her to be strict about was when that agency nurse tried to take over doing the meds.   They were all taken by surprise then.   Celia changed from her calm benign self into a fiend, positively exhaling smoke from her nostrils.

'I am in charge of all the medication in this home and

don't forgot it. In fact don't apply to work here again!' Her neat brown curls shook and her warm face looked pinched and white. They were all really shocked and kept well away from the medicines after that. Generally though, Celia was a very fair boss and work colleague. Sue wondered yet again why she wouldn't join in any out of work social life. Sue pondered. What did she have to go home for? Nobody was there, not even a cat, poor old Pre-med had died a couple of years ago; she had been really upset about that. That worthless husband of hers, Trevor, well he had gone years back, before she had started work at the home. Gossip suggested he had had an affair with another woman, somebody from where he worked Sue thought. Anyway it had been a massive scandal and Celia had been distraught at the time, but Sue was told that everybody was amazed how quickly Celia managed to get back to her old self and maintain her professionalism alongside her warmth with that endearing smile of hers. Evidently Trevor was never seen again or that floozy; people assumed they had run off together. Sue had never talked about it with Celia as chatty as she was, she just wouldn't discuss Trevor. She would give a look with those twinkly blue eyes and smile, but not her normal smile, a tight, slightly curling-lip smile.

Finishing the sheets Sue decided to go and check on a couple of people before tidying up in the kitchen and ending her shift. She had managed to get together about five people for the after work drink in the 'Horse and Groom', which should be a fun half hour. Shame about Celia, she thought, but if she couldn't persuade her to join in. Nobody could. Sue thought she would try again next week.

Celia neatly folded her uniform up and put it in the bag ready to take home for washing and ironing. She liked a fresh uniform every day; a bit excessive she knew, but well, that's just the way she did it. She put on her outdoor coat and got her bag ready, made sure the package was there and checked her purse to make sure she had enough money to buy some fish on the way home. When she got home she put the packages on the kitchen table and unlocked the door into the living room.

'I'm home,' she said as she moved across to unlock the padlocks round his wrists and ankles. 'Time for your medicine and then I will cook us a nice bit of fish for supper.' Trevor looked up at her with his deranged confused eyes and she rewarded him with that endearing smile of hers.

Bitter Lemon

Christina Cummings

My father's cricket hat sits atop a garden spade, more greyish now than white, its brim down-turned with the damp. I could picture the scene: my father digging over the nut-brown soil, tossing earthworms to the brave birds. It would have been a hot day; he would have removed his hat to wipe his brow with the back of his hand, and my mother through the kitchen window would have seized the opportunity to take him a glass of her homemade lemonade, wiping down her lemon scented hands on the front of her apron, slipping the knives and squeezer and cutting board into a bowl of hot water to soak.

She would suggest they drink it on the green porch swing, and would wait for him to sink into the floral cushions, and savour the first sip, before bringing up my name. My father was a reticent man, and it was always wise to strike when he was comfortably settled, too still to wander off, too tranquil to evade. She might have pointed out a flower or perhaps a bee. She would have refilled his glass; the ice-cubes might have made a splash.

'Joe will be visiting this weekend,' my mother would have said.

My father's eyes would cloud. His jaw might have twitched. He would put the glass down with a thud and walk into the house. And with that, he would forget about his hat, as it turned and swayed, like a spinning plate, in the lush afternoon breeze.

The Guy who Spins the Waltzer
Di Reid

It was the late 1950's and Rick was an Elvis Presley look-a-like: swarthy, good looking, slim, black hair, long sideburns, drainpipe trousers, shirt opened to the waist and eyes that penetrated a bra at forty paces.

Rick was seventeen, and his family were part of a group of travelling showmen, taking their Fun Fair to fairgrounds all over the country. From Barnstaple to Birmingham, but now on their way to the Nottingham Goose Fair.

Rick's stamping ground was the Waltzer. When he jumped on the back and spun it round, the local girls screamed and shrieked, skirts billowing upwards, hands pressing downwards, relishing every moment. He could take his pick of them, and often did.

'Isn't he gorgeous?' said Sue to her friend Carol, 'don't you just love his smouldering eyes, and strong arms?'

Rick took his comb out for the hundredth time and combed his hair back seductively, watching the admiring glances. Sue came from a sheltered background, and although instinct told her not to be taken in by him, she found him exciting. She had blonde hair in a ponytail, not backcombed into a beehive like Carol, and she was not allowed to dress in the height of fashion. She had an open fresh looking complexion, snub nose and candid blue eyes, with no make-up except for some pink lipstick of Carol's she had hastily put on, and would soon be rubbing off on the way home. Sue couldn't believe she had lied to her Mum and Dad to get here, but she soon forgot about them.

She loved the Waltzer. In the middle was a brightly painted box where Rick's Dad controlled the platform the cars were on. Up and down, round and round, faster and faster. From this box a myriad coloured lights came out in all directions glittering from the roof, twinkling on the steps leading up to it, and the railings surrounding it. The local boys and girls stood watching, waiting their turn. Music blasted out, and it was the most exciting event of the year.

Sue loved the thrill and spectacle of it all. The dodgems, switchbacks, wall of death, shooting range, amusements, ghost train, roundabouts and swings. The strong man in a leopard skin flexing his muscles, freak shows, and boxing booths where the local lads lost every time. The smell of cheap perfume, candy floss and wet grass. The parading of adolescent bodies in gangs of males and females, strutting their stuff.

Sue watched as Rick jumped nimbly from one car to the other, spinning them round. The girls waiting eagerly for their turn. They jumped in, and were hurled from side to side, clutching each other, screaming, dizzy, and often feeling decidedly sick. The boys trying desperately to look as though this was no big deal, and not convincing anyone.

Rick noticed Sue as she stood out from all the other girls. She was shy and kept looking at him when she thought he didn't see her. Sue didn't flirt with the other boys, and there was an innocence about her that made Rick feel protective and tender towards her. He had never felt like this before.

Sue's father had told her in no uncertain terms to keep away from the fairground. She thought to herself that it had been okay when she was a little girl clutching her candyfloss.

'You keep away my girl. No good will come of it!'

'Oh Dad, everyone else goes, why can't I?'

'Don't argue. I said no and I mean no,' and he looked at her two older brothers Lennie and Joe.

'Don't you two stand there looking gormless, you keep an eye on her.'

Sue looked at her Mum, but there was no support there.

'Do as your Dad says, our Sue. He knows best.'

Rick had girls in every town they visited, but he couldn't

wait to arrive at Sue's town the following year, and see her again. He'd fallen in love. He couldn't stop thinking and dreaming about her. Her smell, her laugh, her perfect body, the shy way she looked at him. She was different from the other tarty looking girls, all heavy make-up, hair back combed to death, and looking and acting as if they were up for it. He was determined that this time he would persuade her to come with him, and they would make a life together.

*

The last time they had visited Nottingham it had taken a long time to convince Sue he was serious, but when he did he was delighted to find she was a virgin. She adored this preening peacock, this exotic creature who turned her stomach upside down, and her legs to jelly. Sex was something she knew nothing about, but being told how beautiful she was, how much he loved her, she lost all her inhibitions. The only time she had been kissed before was at birthday parties playing Postman's Knock.

This was different. Long, lingering kisses, and when Rick put his tongue in her mouth, held her head between his hands, looked into her eyes, and slowly kissed her neck, face and ears she felt like fainting. Sue made a feeble attempt to stop him opening her blouse and expertly taking her bra off, but he silenced her with another long lingering kiss, while he fondled her perfect breasts. She felt alive, and never wanted it to end. He promised to be gentle, and he was, touching her in places that made her feel as eager as he was. Rick quickly took her knickers off, guided her hand to help him with the zip on his trousers. She was surprised at how big he was, but he smothered her in kisses and entered her slowly.

Sue lay back on the damp grass and closed her eyes. She could hear the music of the Waltzer, slow and rhythmic at first, imagined it spinning faster and more out of control, as Rick's urgent and frantic thrustings seemed to be in tune with it, and he reached a moaning climax, drowned out by the shrieks of the girls on the Waltzer as it hurled their bodies around. Despite the noise all around them, the fear of being seen only added to the excitement. She thought she was in heaven as she lay back hugging Rick and looking at the stars. Hurriedly they put their clothes on, and Sue didn't mind the wetness between her legs, and Rick gave her his handkerchief to dry herself. She had been scared, but it had been better than she had been told it would be, and she had enjoyed every second of it. One thing Sue didn't enjoy was telling so many lies to Mum and Dad as to where she was going each night.

It had certainly lacked romance, but she loved Rick and never wanted the week to end. She couldn't wait for the snatched, hurried, passionate moments behind the shooting range each night when Rick was having his break, and she was happier than she had ever been. Sue had felt as though she was walking on air, and smiled dreamily to herself when she thought of his hands on her body. It was her secret, and she never told Carol, who couldn't keep her mouth shut, and would have been so jealous of her.

Lennie and Joe had quite forgotten they were supposed to be keeping an eye on their sister. Rick had asked her to run away from home, and come with him. He would sort it out with his family, knowing they would not be happy about it, and they could have a life travelling together. Sue had thought about this, dreamed about it, but in the end she just did not have the courage, and she loved her family too much to leave them forever.

'I'm sorry,' said Sue on the last passionate night as they clung together. 'I think Dad would kill me, and he would follow me wherever we went and drag me back home.'

Tears had run down her face, and sobs racked her body. She had clung frantically to Rick savouring their last precious moments together, but knowing she had to go quickly before he could change her mind, she had run off before he could stop her. The next day Sue had returned to an empty piece of land. No Waltzer, no gaudy lights, no music blasting out, not even the male, musky scent of Rick. The silence and loneliness engulfed and overwhelmed her, but she had her dreams.

The following year the convoy of trailers, caravans, and cars arrived and they all worked hard setting up the funfair. Rick was so happy, leaping onto the Waltzer, spinning people in their seats, singing with the music, ignoring the girls making eyes at him. Each day and night he looked out for Sue, watching the crowds for that first sight of her. He thought he saw her once in the distance, but he must have been mistaken. On the fifth day he was packing up for the night, and walking back to his caravan, distracted by thoughts of Sue, and wondering where she was. He didn't have time off to look for her, but he just knew she would turn up. It was dark, lights out, the fairground quiet at last, when he heard a noise. He turned in time to see a baseball bat swinging towards his head.

'That's for our Sue,' said Lenny, and Sue was the last word Rick heard as he lapsed into unconsciousness. Lenny, Joe, and their Dad kicked at Rick's inert body, and then made their way back home.

Sue's Dad had waited patiently for this day, ever since Sue announced she was pregnant at the age of sixteen. Her mum had worked out the dates, but she wouldn't say who the father was despite threats, her mum's tears, and her father ranting on for days.

'Lennie, Joe, what the hell were you two idle bastards doing? You were supposed to be watching out for her.'

'Sorry Dad,' they said as they tried to dodge the inevitable clip around the ear.

When the baby was born they all looked at the spitting image of Rick. Sue's cries, protests and pleading were to no avail and he was put up for adoption.

When the fair came to town Dad made Sue point Rick out, then she was guarded night and day until she could be sent off to Auntie Joan's in Wales for a month.

Rick survived for two days, but never regained consciousness. His family were distraught, and vowed revenge, but against who? The police were convinced it was a vendetta between the travellers and they lost interest, and the fair moved on.

The London in Me

I talk London in my heart,
I hear London with each step,
I walk London with the world
and in this village of everyone,
I am at home.

I am smaller in the crowd,
faster in the eternal city,
focused and intent on walking
as I move through time
from stucco to glass.

So many people's purposes;
self-possessed silences
and yet, there is a subtle intimacy.
There are recognitions and
connections, tenderness and
an awareness of kindness and
friendship and the past's
echoing present where I am
with you again, standing next to
bright water,
sparkling in the sun;
lost in memories

and found in the streets -
Rosslyn Hill, Finchley Rd,
Canfield Gardens,
Shaftsbury Avenue -
that hold the secrets
of my youth.

The music in the subways
sets the beat before my feet
and I rise on moving stairs
through an archway into air,
where I am breathing in the
strangeness, garlanded by
Chinese lanterns, dressed by
fashion houses and laughed
by children, as we walk
in the heart of the city.

Hilary Gregory

Pas de Deux

Jenny McRobert

This was the moment. The once-in-a–lifetime-you-will-never-forget-it moment. I knew it, and so did Barbara.

We had queued for twenty-four hours solid. It was the only way to be sure of tickets for the whole season. Covent Garden was a fruit and vegetable market then, our sleeping bags laid down among mashed cabbage leaves, discarded apples and other rotting, unrecognisable bits and pieces. But, it was not bad. It smelled earthy and mellow. Cheery men would go past, pushing barrows laden with orange boxes and offer us fresh fruit, and even the occasional exotic delicacy like peaches or mangoes.

During the day Floral Street belonged to smart people clutching briefcases, hurrying to work. Skinny kids with turned out toes scurrying to and from ballet school. Burly men loading huge pieces of scenery through the side entrance, performers, famous and aspiring, sauntering through the stage door.

But at night the streets belonged to the costermongers - the kings and queens of fruit and veg.

Mum and Dad were never sure that two teenaged girls would be safe queuing all night. Dad had the embarrassing habit of turning up just after midnight, to make sure we were okay. We were more than okay. The colourful, cultured slice of humanity, the ballet and opera nuts, the failed would-be performers ... they were all there and they all had a tale to tell. No one really slept. We would take it in shifts, covering someone's spot while they went off for a break to a coffee bar or the Wimpy.

That year we had been particularly lucky. Securing our place in the front four of the queue, we got seats for the whole season in the front row of the amphitheatre, and that included the world premier of the ballet Romeo and Juliet with Fonteyn and Nureyev. We were both madly in love with Nureyev, oblivious to any hint about his sexual preferences that might make him less of a 'dreamboat' to fourteen and seventeen year old sisters.

On the night of the premiere we were in heaven. We took our seats among the plush red velvet and lavish gold cherubs. The orchestra tuning sounded like multiple choirs of humming bees, making the air vibrate. It was thrilling when the heavy curtain bearing the Royal Opera House insignia was finally raised to reveal graceful dancers kitted out in glittering, colourful costumes dancing out an impossible life in an impossibly glamorous world. But it was magic.

There was always a thrill when Rudolph leapt on the stage. He seemed to hang in the air ... feeding the illusion that he could float forever, until *he* decided to touch down. His presence was electric, he owned the stage. More than that, he set it alight with the force of his personality and his talent.

After the show we waited outside the stage door, just to catch a glimpse of our idols. Dame Margot appeared, always elegant and polite, a gentle smile on her lips as she bid us all good evening. Finally, came Rudolph, looking beautiful in a black leather jacket, his fair hair slightly tousled, carrying a huge bouquet of flowers ... and that's when it happened.

We had Russian grandparents and had both taken a fancy to learning the language in an evening class. Barbara was much more proficient than me and, as Rudy swept by her with his usual intent of 'getting the hell out of here as soon as possible' some people cried out 'Rudy, Rudy, let's have your autograph.'

Rudy replied 'I not sign, not for no-one.' Then Barbara quietly said 'poshalusta' (please in Russian). Rudy turned and looked at her. His face softened into a warm smile and they exchanged a few words in Russian. Rudy signed her programme then said to my sister, 'Tonight I walk. You walk with me. We talk.'

I tagged along feeling invisible but not minding in the least. I looked up at Rudy as we walked. He chatted with my sister about films he'd enjoyed, countries he had visited, people he knew. His breath smelled of champagne. His leather jacket felt warm and soft as I touched his arm lightly. He looked down at me, puzzled for a moment, as if he had not known I was there. Then he carried on his intense conversation with Barbara. I did not mind, my mouth was dry, my tongue was tied, my heart beat wildly ... I did not want to talk.

When we reached Leicester Square, Rudolph decided he had had enough walking. He signalled to his driver, who had been crawling along in the Rolls Royce beside us.

Before he left, he looked at Barbara, smiled and handed her his huge bunch of flowers. 'This is for you pretty girl ... Dosvedanya.'

We stood in silence as we watched him go, neither of us wanting to break the spell.

Carbuncles and Marigolds
Kirsty Whittle

It's a simmering July day outside. If I tilt my head a little I can see the Year 10 netball team out in the sun, doing that catching and swivelling thing that I've never mastered, deftly looping the ball through the nets. They laugh, the golden girls, glistening in the heat and Miss Pike blows her whistle and smiles and claps a couple of casual claps the way sports people do, though when *I* play netball she just scowls like a hot cat and shakes her head.

Back in the classroom though, it doesn't feel like July. It might as well be January as Mr Scott drones on about the Magna Carta with his back turned towards us, pointing up at his interminable notes on the whiteboard.

I think, if I hold my breath, perhaps I can make July last forever. School will end on the 23rd and we will bask in the knowledge that the holidays are spread out before us, wide as an ocean. And August will never come with its shoes-and-stationery shopping trips, and neither will September, so we'll never have to drag ourselves back here again.

Only another half hour to go. I'll meet Ash at the gates and he'll wink at me and grab my hand with his oil-paint stained fingers and he'll smell of Burnt Umber and Prussian Blue. We'll walk into town and it'll feel like school never happened.

It'll be Ash's birthday on the fifteenth. Star sign: Cancer.

What I wouldn't give to be star sign Cancer.

If I was, I'd be a better person. Like Ash.

I Googled it. Symbol: the crab. Moody. Sensitive. Empathic. Element: water. Ruling planet: the Moon. Closest metal: silver. Lucky colour: silver-grey. Lucky gems: opal, pearl and moonstone. Basic trait: *I feel*.

And that is just Ash all over. He is opal, pearl and moonstone. He paints. He loves. He feels.

I, on the other hand, sitting in this classroom with the most boring teacher in the world, am stuck with August.

Star sign: Leo. Egotistic. Energetic. Prone to jealousy. Element: fire. Ruling planet: the Sun. Closest metal: gold. Lucky gems: diamonds and carbuncles. (Carbuncles??!!) Lucky flower: marigolds. Basic trait: *I will*.

See what I mean? How did I end up a Leo? I look again at the netball players: *they* are Leo, with their glowing goal celebrations and their diamond-cut hearts and their *can do* attitudes. I am neither Leo *nor* Cancer. Neither July *nor* August. I am lost somewhere in between.

But I will go out into the sunshine after school and I will hold hands with opal, pearl and moonstone. I will feel the silver. I will smell the Burnt Umber and the Prussian Blue. And I will squeeze myself as close to July as I can.

Travels with Yankee Stellar
Angela Ramsell

I know now why the Americans call their satellite navigation systems GPS. It's because they make no attempt to navigate you anywhere.

We picked up the hire car from Logan Airport, Boston, USA and we also picked up a GPS system.

'That's good Ken. It's a Garmin, the same make as I have at home so that should make things easier.'

Famous last words. We were aiming for a place called Kittery, about 60 miles north of Boston, but located in Maine. Boston is in the state of Massachusetts - this happily meant we could avoid Boston completely. We found the car, loaded our luggage and I familiarised myself with the controls and then we got out the GPS, plugged it in and I pressed the 'Where to' button. Up popped a screen with a touch keyboard, just like at home. I typed in Kittery and pressed 'Done' and waited. A list of all the Kitterys in the USA appeared. I scrolled down eagerly, but was there a Kittery, ME to be seen? No way.

Ten minutes later, after consulting the map and a great deal of bad language, I had managed to get it to recognise,

Portsmouth, New Hampshire, just across the river from Kittery.

'That's as good as it gets Ken, so we'll have to settle for that.'

'Well if you're sure.'

'We don't have any alternative and I'm sure there'll be road signs to Kittery.'

I started up the car, reversed out of the parking space and exited the car hire lot.

The GPS was saying insistently, 'Please drive to highlighted route.' Problem was, there was no route highlighted on the screen and definitely no highlighted road. I turned left, which seemed the obvious way to go and the highlighted road appeared, showing me I should have turned right.

'Recalculating. Drive to next junction and turn right,' commanded the box.

This I did.

'Carry straight on and take the next turning left.'

Following 'she who must be obeyed' to the letter, I turned left at the next junction and found myself in a car park. There was no sound of encouragement or disgust from Ken, in fact he appeared to be completely speechless.

'Oh blow!' (I would have used stronger language here, if I'd been on my own.) 'I'll have to turn left here or we'll end up going through the barrier!'

'Okay, if you think you can.'

This I did and exited the car park.

'Recalculating. Turn right 200 yards ahead.'

I did this and found myself on one of the airport roads . Almost immediately the GPS said, 'Turn right here.' I was in the left lane and couldn't move over. I looked at the road sign overhead. 'Sumner Tunnel to Boston,' it said.

'Oh shit, we're going into Boston, Ken!'

No response. He was looking quite pale and staring fixedly ahead.

'Recal... ' the GPS voice went silent as we went deeper into the tunnel and a little sign appeared on the screen.

'It's lost contact with the satellite.' A voice of doom spoke from the seat next to me.

'Bloody good job too. If I used the road signs instead of listening to that thing we wouldn't be driving into Boston now!'

Deeper and deeper under the earth we went and then we started to go up. The signs overhead told me that the Government Centre was straight ahead.

'Oh God, we're coming out right in the centre of Boston, Ken.'

Silence. I looked across at him, he was as white as a sheet of A4 printing paper and was clutching the edge of his seat so tightly his knuckles had turned white. I began to worry that I might have to start looking for a hospital, rather than the way out of Boston.

We emerged from the tunnel into blinding sunlight.

'Quick, it's telling us to turn right here.'

'Ken, I'm, not listening to that thing anymore, I'm going to use the road signs. If I go straight ahead, that sign says to turn left for Portsmouth and the north.'

'Well if you're sure you want to do that.'

'I'm certain that that's what I want to do.'

Five minutes later we were over the bridge and negotiating our way on to the Interstate, which would take us to Portsmouth. The GPS had been stopped and silence reigned. All was well with the world inside the car.

We got to Portsmouth, found the sign to Kittery and arrived in time for a coffee and then we hit the shops.

After we'd finished and were back in the car, there was no choice we had to use the GPS to take us to our hotel in Dover - not by the sea I might add, but very close to Andover and

Salisbury. This time, 'Yankee Stellar', as I'd named her, was feeling quite mellow and found our destination straight away, navigating us there without any problems. She obviously enjoyed the retail therapy.

Yes, she had to come everywhere with us, the assistant at the car hire office had threatened with pain of death if we left her behind. She was not a little thing to carry around either, because she was fixed to a nice little weighted skirt to hold her on the dashboard and came complete with a bright yellow bag, the size of a lunchbox to carry her in.

I later found out that it wasn't just the retail therapy that made her feel mellow, she definitely preferred country roads and almost purred when she gave directions on these, but appeared to bark out instructions when we were in towns and cities and quite often failed to notify me of turnings. There again, maybe it was me that failed to hear the instructions. Of course I put the blame entirely on her. What did she know sitting up there on her satellite trying to find a small, white car on the big, busy, American roads?

The Train

The golden hue, the flashes of light
Stream by on the train tonight
Cutting its way 'cross fields through
Towns eating up the land all around

Racing the cars on the auto route
It's the train that wins, hear the toot
Anticipation ... clickety clack
What's waiting at the end of the track?

People around lost in their thoughts
Some with music, some in a book
Catch a quick glance, steal a look,
We're in it together and yet on our own

Someone coughs, a baby howls
A child wriggles, a grown up snores
Up to the buffet, gaze out at the view
Fellow passengers just do what they do

The Train – Sally Thompson

Some want time to pass quickly away
But oh no not me, I savour this day
My very first ride on such a fast train
As it rolls and whooshes and takes the strain

We're each in our bubble of memories forgot
Despite all the noises so loud and then not
Where have you come from, where have you been?
Are you looking forward to what's still to be seen?

We're slowing now, the sky-line has changed
Snow capped mountains ahead fill the space
The mind wanders off into a dream of the days
Ahead with our images to seek and amaze

How will it go with the new folks we meet?
The train that's carried us pulls to a stop
It shakes us awake with a jolt and a rock
The journey's ended, it's time to get up.

Sally Thompson

When Your Number's Up
Gill Johnson

'Cornflakes or Coco Rocks?' She remembered banging both boxes on the table.

As Sue bunched fresh cut flowers from the garden, she played over and over again that breakfast on the television of her mind. She pushed the stems into the vase, added sprigs of rosemary and shuffled them into a stable arrangement. Rosemary for remembrance. Her memories pulled her back into the past again.

*

'Cornflakes or Coco Rocks?' shouted Ellie, bouncing up and down in the chair with the enthusiasm of a six year old so early in the morning.

'Rocks,' echoed James, her nearly five year old brother, banging his spoon on the table. 'Rocks and rolls, like daddy.'

'I want my Dalmatian bowl,' demanded Ellie getting down from her chair to rummage in the cupboard.

'Careful, Ellie,' Sue leaned over her, opened the cupboard door to find her children's favourite cereal bowls and then took them to the table and poured out the required amount.

'More,' demanded James. 'More, more.'

'I'd like some more please. But no, James. Eat this first and then we'll see.'

She slopped milk into both the bowls and handed the children their spoons to encourage them to eat.

Biting a piece of toast, she attacked yesterday's crockery in the dishwasher and crashed it away in various cupboards, before refilling the machine with the evening and early morning detritus that had gathered on the kitchen top.

'Any tea?' Alex had come into the room, tying his tie, and kissed Sue on the top of her head. He smelt of toothpaste and shaving foam and looked cool and smart in his cotton shirt.

'Hello kiddiwids,' he turned to the children.

'Dad, Dad,' they shouted as he gave each a kiss ignoring their milky faces and accepted a mug of tea from the obliging Sue.

'What do snowmen eat for breakfast?' he asked them.

'Ice krispies,' Ellie shouted, well versed on this favourite joke.

'Frosties,' shouted James with the usual alternate answer.

Sue sighed and popped some toast on a plate and put it in front of Alex.

'Quarter to,' she warned him and turned to put the children's sandwiches in their lunch bags.

Popping another piece of toast in her mouth she buried herself in the tumble drier and filling her arms with warm clothes, she threw the heap on the table, extricating two pairs of shorts from the muddle.

'What do you say when you meet a two headed monster?' Alex asked the children, waving the two pairs of shorts over his head as monster masks.

They shook their heads.

'Dunno,' said Ellie.

'Hello, hello!'

Sue meanwhile had emptied the contents of the washing machine into the tumble drier, refilled the washing machine and clicked both on, checking for the swoosh and whir.

Returning to the breakfast table, where splodges of milk littered the surface and half-filled bowls of soggy cereal had been abandoned, the children's attention had been turned to soldiers Alex had made them with his toast.

'Like Daddy,' James said with a buttery grin.

'Ten minutes,' Sue warned.

'I can count to a hundred,' James shouted. 'Listen, Dad. 1, 2 miss a few, 99, 100.' He threw his head back and guffawed loudly. Alex ruffled his head.

'Yes, but can you count what's in between?'

'1, 2345678,' began James.

'Hurry up you two,' Sue began to feel that she was the only one with a grip on reality. 'Nearly eight o'clock and Daddy has to get the train. Uncle Ben is going up to London with him today, he'll be on the train too.'

'I love Uncle Ben,' Ellie smiled.

'Come on Ellie - teeth clean now. James.'

Sue took Ellie upstairs.

'20, 21, 22 ...'

'James.'

Ellie plodded up the stairs. '1, 2 miss a few 99, 100. We have a hundred steps, Mum.'

'Teeth clean now!'

'34, 35, 36 ...'

'James.'

Sue bustled in the bathroom, Ellie, compliant, let Sue brush her teeth, wipe her sticky mouth and then went to the loo.

'88, 89, 90 ...'

'James.'

'91, 92 ... ' The counting got louder as Alex, with James wrapped around him, climbed the stairs.

'99,100.'

'Excellent, young chap, now teeth!'

Sue picked him off Alex.

'Oh look, now you've a butter smear on your tie.'

'Never mind,' said Alex, 'got plenty of clean ones, I'll tie it in the car.'

'We've got to go,' Sue insisted.' Turning to Ellie, 'Sweetheart, go downstairs and put your coat on.' Sue pushed James into the bathroom and supervised his hurried ablutions and herded him downstairs.

Gathering her own bag from the bedroom she found Alex dithering over two ties.

'Which one?' he asked.

'The blue,' she said without looking – he had several blue ties. 'It's 5 past 8.'

Rushing past James on the stairs with a quick 'Hurry up', Sue went to collect the lunch bags from the kitchen.

'Are your coats on?' she called.

Ellie was waiting by the door, coat on but somehow upside down. Sue sighed and removed it helping her to put it on correctly. James was now sitting down playing with a car.

'I'm James Bond and this is my car- vrooommmm.'

'James, shoes,' ordered Sue.

'Mum, watch my car. Vroooooooom.'

'No, James, let's get your shoes on. Daddy has to catch the train.' Sue could feel heat rising up from her back to her face as she struggled to put the shoes on James' feet.

'James Bond is in his car, chasing nasty men.'

Sue pushed the shoes on the unyielding feet. 'I'm sure James Bond has shoes on,' enticed Sue.

'I've got shoes on,' stated Ellie proudly.

'Good girl, Ellie,' encouraged Sue.

'Lovely car – Ace spy car,' Alex helped by picking James up. 'I'll put him in the car, you lock up.' He turned to his young son. 'When you get older and earn loads of money you can buy a real one of these, James.' Alex's voice tailed off as they hurried out.

'Come on Ellie,' said Sue, 'Let's go.'

Finally all were in the car and snapped into their seats when James let out a wail.

'No car. I've lost my car.'

Alex looked at Sue, opened the door, leapt out and searched the driveway. There was no sign of the car.

'Give me the keys,' he held out his hand to Sue, who had already turned on the ignition in her position as driver. Sue rummaged in her bag and gave the house keys to Alex.

'Hurry up,' she called after his retreating back.

Alex let himself in the house and found the car by the door on the mat inside. Picking it up, he locked the door and was back in the car.

Sue revved up and pointed the car in the direction of the station.

Ten minutes before the 8:25 she noted by the clock in the car.

Like every day the same songs were sung in the car and as Sue turned into the station car park they were all singing the loud chorus of 'The Animal Stampede.'

'It's a stampede- the animals were freed

Scattering, smattering in the dash,

Through the jungle- hear the CRASH.'

Following two slow cars, Sue pushed the vehicle up the ramp to the station entrance and stopped to let Alex out. Bending across the front of the car Alex gave her a kiss and blew one each to James and Ellie sitting upright in their child seats.

'See you all tonight, pumpkins,' and with a wave disappeared into the station entrance.

Sue put the car into gear to deliver the children to their school, then on to collect the dry cleaning, the post that had not been left due to a signature being needed and onto the supermarket. It was almost 10:30 when she returned home to the remains of the breakfast bash and the laundry. Sighing, she switched on the radio, never realising that by doing so the table would remain uncleared and the laundry left undone that day. The terrible news was told in a solemn voice as part of the broadcast.

*

Sue shook her memories away and shuffling the sprigs of rosemary, stepped back to look at the display. She felt a tiny hand slip into hers and she looked down at Ellie who was carrying some stems.

'Put them in the bowl,' Sue told her and watched her little fingers fumble with the flowers. James came up and wrapped his arms around her waist. The panic, inexplicable, began to rise from the pit of her stomach again, threatening to envelop her whole being.

'One two, miss a few 99, 100,' she breathed to herself. She opened her eyes and looked at James.

He had his favourite Aston Martin car in his hands.

'I'm giving this,' he said and put it by the flowers. Sue felt tears begin to roll down her eyes. The car was important to all of them, an important part of the memory of that breakfast and the rush to catch the 8:25 train. The fatal train that had crashed - wreckage of lives and loves.

'I think that's a good idea,' said Sue, hugging her children close.

'Mummy,' asked James. 'Where's Daddy?'

Sue turned to her children and kissed them both as they stood before the grave.

'I'm here,' Alex came up behind them his eyes red and his face white.

He looked at the car and at Sue.

'That car made me miss the train,' he said.

Sue nodded. 'Perhaps it's only fitting that Uncle Ben should have it now.'

May – My Best Friend
Marjorie Andrews

May and I have known each other for years. Our mothers were friends and we lived round the corner from each other, all our lives. My parents had a small – or as they would say, a refined guest house in a small seaside town in the south of England. May's parents ran the off-licence shop in the next road. Our mothers met at the Mother and Baby Clinic when collecting their Clinic orange juice and cod liver oil.

We were born in 1942, she in May and me in September. I'm typical Virgo, being extremely tidy and self-sufficient and some would say perhaps a little stubborn. May has all the characteristics of the Taurus sign being jolly, placid and a very good friend.

We are now both in our late 60's. May is divorced and I have never married. I have never wanted to. May trained as a hairdresser and I helped my mother and father run the guest house until they both died. I sold the guest house and bought myself a very nice flat overlooking the sea. I absolutely love it and wake up every morning thinking just how lucky I am.

May and I meet every Wednesday, at the afternoon tea dance, in a hotel along the front. It's looking a bit jaded these days, because it has lost some of its sparkle, as have most of the hotels. All it needs is a lick of paint. But it's slowly starting to come back to life, as families are suddenly realising that small seaside towns have a lot to offer.

One Wednesday May came into the dance hall, I can only describe it as "strutting", with such confidence that, for a moment, I felt a little jealous. She looked absolutely stunning, but I couldn't quite make out why. She always looks nice but, this day, she looked a bobby dazzler.

We are a bit short of men at the tea dances, so the women often dance together. One or two middle aged couples have started to join the dance lessons, as these are provided free, along with the very nice tea they give us. We are a mixed bunch; there is the grey army, people in their late 50's, all looking for something to do on a Wednesday afternoon. What makes it special is a nice young man who plays the records. He is so respectful to us old folks and also very patient when teaching us difficult steps. The highlight of the afternoons is when he teaches us to Salsa. What a treat that is, when a young man struts his stuff!

Anyway, when May and I were practising our Fox Trot, I accidentally trod on her toes. She stopped dead in her tracks and said to me, 'If you tread on my toes once more, I will clock you one.'

I was absolutely astounded, both at her manner and what she said to me.

'Haven't you seen what I have got on my feet?'

'To be honest I hadn't.'

On her feet were the most beautiful dance shoes I have ever seen in my life. They were silver, with crystal encrusted high heels and, peeking out of her shoes on her big toe, would you believe, a tattoo of a bee. To say I was lost for words ... well.

She then spoke to me in this cocky manner.

'While you're at it have a look at my eyes and lips – I have had those done as well.'

I just had to go and sit down.

She followed me and apologised.

'Sorry, love, I was peeved because you hadn't noticed my shoes. They are Jimmy Choos, you know.'

I told her, that I wouldn't know Jimmy Choo or any other fashionable footwear if I fell over them. I knew she looked different, but hadn't quite fathomed what it was, until the incident of treading on her toes. As for the tattooed eyelids and lips - something's happening here.

We both sat down to our afternoon tea and she told me how she had acquired such amazing dance slippers, also why she had had the tattoos. It was nothing more than just wanting to be different from the person she thought she had become - boring.

We had not seen each other for two weeks as the hotel was booked for a private tea dance. Because of this May had volunteered for an extra day at the charity shop. She worked there two days a week. I did my charity bit by fund raising for my local church, so we both felt we were giving something back to society with our extra days.

She told me that on the afternoon of her extra Wednesday an elderly gentleman had come into the shop carrying the most enormous hold-all which was made by the fashion design house 'Burberry'. Then she told me what had happened.

This gent had come into the shop just before lunchtime. He seemed very sad and distant in his approach. She gave him a smile and asked could she help.

He replied, 'I am absolutely distraught. My wife died a couple of days ago. We'd been on holiday, having travelled all the way from Australia for nostalgic reasons.'

She sat him down and asked would he like a cup of coffee. She closed the shop early in order to talk to him properly, and make him a cup of coffee. She said he was welcome to share some of her sandwiches. He declined, but said coffee would be very acceptable.

She described him as 'late sixties, average height, very up-together, but most of all, he smelt like a sea breeze.' She said he intoxicated her and was shocked at her reaction to this stranger. They'd had their coffee and then he'd said, 'Would you like to see what I would like to leave with you. I can't bear to take them back home with me and I am sure my wife would like them to go to a good home.'

First out of the bag came a shoe box. And in the shoe box were little silk bags, and in each bag was a shoe.

May said, 'I couldn't believe what I was seeing. Brand new silver sandals with crystal encrusted heels and from the soles they looked as though they had never been worn. There were some lovely clothes, very simple, tasteful and beautifully packed in tissue paper.' May said she felt it was like trespassing into somebody's private life.

'Don't say anything, please, please, just take them.'

He got up to go and, as went through the door, adding 'I'm here for another week. Would you be so kind to have dinner with me tomorrow evening? You choose where we go, as you probably know better than me where to eat. I would like you to have the shoes because they are special and you have been so kind to me.'

May told me she nearly telephoned to ask my advice about going out for dinner with a man she had only just met. She'd chickened out as she thought I would say she was mad and tell her he might be a philanderer, that he could have even done this before in order to get to know women of a certain age; or, at the very worst might be a serial killer.

Then she dropped her bombshell.

'I shan't be coming dancing for some time and I hope you won't be cross with me or think I am disloyal, but I am going to Australia for a holiday in two weeks time to see William.'

Shocked and surprised.

'If the bar is open, I should like a brandy and you can bloody well pay for it!'

And May did just that.

Six months have gone by and May's coming home to sort things out. She's going to marry William eventually, when all the paperwork is done. She's not selling up because if she ever wants to come back she will have somewhere to live.

She has asked me if I will take care of her home as a holiday let. It will be a big responsibility, but she is my friend, so I agreed. Something to keep me occupied, as I shall miss her so much.

Two years have passed and May is coming home - the surprise is that we are both going to need somebody to look after our homes as I am going back with her for the holiday of a lifetime. We are stopping off in Dubai for a few days, where we plan to have the biggest spending spree of our lives. May is going to marry Will. He has asked her many times and, at last, she has agreed.

Guess what? She wants me to be her bridesmaid.

We both fly out tomorrow. We are so excited, just like the times when we were teenagers looking for the man of our dreams. May had married at twenty but it didn't work out. Maybe, because she is older and wiser, this one will.

I hope so.

You never know, I might meet the man of my dreams and it might be fate that I have to go across the world to find him. I will certainly let you know.

On Writing the Village Pantomime

The village pantomime is bound to be sublime
In couplets it must rhyme (so actors learn their lines ...)

We start with the hero, the prince we esteem
Handsome and daring, most manly it would seem.
But can it be true, my head's in a whirl,
The prince in a panto is played by a girl?
The one stipulation – she must have good pins
For the briefest of shorts when the panto begins.

Then there's the princess, beautiful and fair
The one with whom the prince will want to share
The rest of his life within minutes of meeting
Though they've barely done more than exchange their
                                      first greeting.
The action will thrust them apart and together
Through trials, tribulations, all stormy weather.

On Writing the Village Pantomime – Madeleine Woosnam

Which brings us to the baddy, key to the plot
A giant, a witch, a demon king, heaven knows what?
All of them ugly, sinister, greedy and cruel
To frighten the kiddies and provide a good duel.
So baddies aplenty are usually the score
One is essential but often there are more.

A fairy we must have for sparkle and glitter
To help our brave heroes and raise the odd titter.
She represents good while he is the evil.
(They sometimes have armies of very small people.)
Together they're 'immortals' and balance each other
From stage right and left, like sister and brother.

There's always a dame, usually a man
With vast, heaving bosom, large bloomers and fan
Mostly she's the mother, ugly sister or cook
A widow, a spinster but never a crook.
A tuneless falsetto must be well employed
To make eyes at the baddy she'll then be deployed.
(The men in our village all like to wear frocks
So it's nuns, bearded ladies and long flowing locks.)

On Writing the Village Pantomime – Madeleine Woosnam

And sometimes a simpleton, a clown or a fool,
A brother for our hero, for us to ridicule.
Like Buttons in Cinders or Idle Jack in Dick
Whatever the panto he's never that quick.
He leads the audience, yet pretends not to hear
Their calling and shouting each time he appears.

Dozens of children will overrun the stage.
Don't take on animals, although it's the rage,
Unless they have two ends, a back and a front
A pantomime cow, or camel with hump.
The kids will play fairies, munchkins and rats,
Animals, dwarves, gypsies and cats.
A song and a line then it's straight home to bed
Dad's got the video and there's backstage tears shed.

So ... parts for the teenagers (they all must have lines)
And flattering costumes (to avoid ghastly whines).
A cameo role for the vicar include
Just make quite sure that it's not too rude
Parts for the tall, the short, fat and lean
Parts for the old, young and those in between
Parts for the gifted, and oh it's so galling,
There must also be parts for the frankly appalling.

On Writing the Village Pantomime – Madeleine Woosnam

The songs should be short and very well known
(The words can be changed to lower the tone.)
Some sung tunefully, others a dirge
Some, the director will mercifully purge.
A chorus adds energy, colour and shine
If only they'd bloody remember their lines.

Custard pies, slapstick and terrible gags
Kings, queens and monsters, disgusting old hags,
Men dressed as women, women as men
Suddenly here we are, at it again.
In jokes, innuendo, rude noises, all these
Are essential ingredients of Pantomimese.

With 'Oh no it won't' and 'Oh yes it will'
The audience must shout 'till they've had their fill.
They all like a bit of loud participation
It helps keep their minds off the rate of inflation.
They love a good singsong it's really essential.
(You never know where you may spot new potential.)

On Writing the Village Pantomime – Madeleine Woosnam

The panto progresses. The good win the day
And everyone gets just desserts on the way.
Our prince and princess in marriage united
A touching love song when their troth is plighted.
Miraculously everyone gets coupled at last
And all must admit that the show's been a blast.

I feel quite exhausted on reading this through
I've no doubt that probably you do too
But in spite of all this, I have to confess
A certain excitement, though I must not digress.
At the thought of blank pages that wait to be filled
With all of those characters whose life I'll have willed.

So pity my family who must laugh at my jokes
(My girls would rather be out seeing blokes)
And play second fiddle when sometimes it seems
My characters are real, not merely my dreams.
And supper's been burnt, the washing not done
But it's ok cos I'm having such jolly good fun.
Never mind I forget to collect them from school
My children think writing a panto is cool.

On Writing the Village Pantomime – Madeleine Woosnam

Dorothy's dusting off her slippers again.
My head's full of scarecrows, lions, tin men
Of witches and munchkins who wait to rehearse
The pages I'm writing of songs, jokes and verse.
The rhyming dictionary's never far from my hand
The panto tradition is the finest in the land!

ENCORE!

The village pantomime is bound to be sublime
In couplets it must rhyme - time for a glass of wine ...

CURTAIN

Madeleine Woosnam

Our Last Day in Amazonia
Carole Hastings

Today I visited Kusutkan, an Achuar village in the Ecuadorean rainforest, two week's walk from so-called civilisation. This week, Simon our guide from this village has accompanied us on all our treks. The respect I feel for this man is immense. On the vast Pastaza River, he has called up Pink River Dolphins by imitating the sound of their young. He has identified birds so far from normal sight that it is clear why he is known as Harpy Eagle. He has shown us how to make animal traps, blow-pipes and spears from palm trees in order to eat meat. He has shown us the plants and trees from which he makes medicines to relieve sickness, headaches, muscle fatigue and even stem a bleeding wound. He has told us of his rites of passage that made him the strong and centred man he is today. He has taken us to the Achuar's sacred places – a gentle waterfall and a massive tree whose buttressed roots could house four families. These places have exuded a peace and holiness to match any cathedral.

Kapawi lodge, where we have been staying, has been given to the Achuar people on whose land it stands. The villages receive a small fee for allowing guests to visit them and this visit was pure business. It revealed a slice of life that bears no relation to our own. The chief's wife made her manioc beer, handicrafts and cooking pots. The chief, eying us in a bemused fashion, made a beautiful comb whilst answering our questions about the problems that face his community today.

These native hunter-gatherers are in the throes of learning a new skill set. Their challenge is how to run Kapawi as a profitable business, without harming the rainforest and the way of life of the only Indian community in Ecuador who have not succumbed to the oilmen's dollar. The chief knows that 60% of Ecuador's economy is based on oil and some day someone will try to make the Achuar an offer they will struggle to refuse, if they cannot make this fundamental leap of a lifetime. We all sat there in the steaming jungle heat knowing that the Achuar way of life hangs on a thread.

The Achuar families have all they need to live stress-free and simple lives – an oil strike would change that overnight. Reflecting on the clutter and nonsense we have in our lives I am minded of Ghandi's words when he visited a department store in England many years ago, "I didn't know there were so many things I didn't need."

It was strange to leave the village knowing that, as with all the Achuar men who work at Kapawi - one month on/one month off - Simon will return to his village next month and really use his blow pipe and traps to provide food for his family. In our society we talk of juggling our lives – we really don't know the meaning of those words ...

Reflections

Sonja Eagle

The luminous sea reflects shadows from the early summer sun and small crystals of light play in the air fusing with my thoughts. I pull the cover over my knees as even in the sunshine there is a slight coolness with the wind and in my now delicate state any chill could make me worse. The sea looks glowing as the sun plays on the splashing water and delicate sprays of white lacy froth beat down into the vigorous repetition. What a wonderful spectacle of nature, relentless in its comings and goings, with the ability to change from an azure calm and then again into a raging grey, angry tyrant.

As I close my eyes and reflect on my long life, I can see days of happiness on the beach, with first my children, and then their children. The shouting over the noise of the waves, the laughter of fallen sandcastles, the crying of small quarrels. The hurly burly of life condensed into a family day out, all overseen by the anguished screech of the seagulls circling above.

As I drift further back, I remember on this part of the beach, resolutely playing and trying to show how happy I was to be there, with my mother waving at me every time she looked up to check I was still alright. Hiding from me, the tears in her eyes, trying so hard to smile and pretend all was going to be the same. It wasn't of course with dad missing in action; it couldn't ever be the same. We were used to being alone, my mum, my sister and I. But we weren't used to knowing he would never come home again. And he didn't. Years later we found out he had been torpedoed and his ship had gone down with all men on board. Claimed by the cruel sea and taken to his watery grave.

I can see young lovers walking hand in hand on the water's edge laughing and playing with the tide as it splashes their feet. To them the sea is exciting and benign as indeed it should be as they excitedly go forward into their lives. I wish them well, I wish them health and happiness but above all I wish them the variety my life has brought to me.

It's such a comfort to know the sea will obey the moon and continue to pound ceaselessly long after my life has expired.

Pear Season

Christina Cummings

Footsteps trail away down the stairs and along the hall carpet. 'If you need anything ... ' he says as he lifts the latch. Birdsong and strangers' voices carry from the pavement, filtering up to my bedroom, as the front door opens momentarily. And then, he's gone.

Tucking the latest prescription beneath a jar of violet-scented cold cream, I run my fingers over the dresser, leaving tiger stripes in a soft layer of dust. A tarnished mirror looks back at me. Through the gauzy reflection, I see myself both ten years younger and ten years older. In the one, I see myself in summer dress, laughing over a dining table, a white wine glass tilted up to toast, my mouth leaning in to kiss. In the other, I am scuttling, bent and breathless, fussing over fat tabby cats as I take to my armchair to watch the soaps. I know in this moment that all I have is now. I know that my soft skinned days have peeled away, as time, with slow-slippered feet, propels me inexorably from youth.

I tug at the belt of my towelling dressing gown, until it hugs me, and turn my face to the window. Sunlight bathes the pear tree and scatters onto the tufted lawn below, where next door's cat yawns; his high arched back a semi-colon in the grass. He lies upturned now, unfazed by the squawking, flapping, greasy feathered crows that bounce on a high-wire, which trails from the telegraph poles connecting these tidy houses, like a child's dot-to-dot. And then I see her - Mary's granddaughter, framed by the window. She holds a lipstick in the air like a single rose and twirls the stem. With a deliberate sweep, she smears her lips, her face bright with expectation. I recall how when she'd visited last year, she'd gathered fallen pears and lined them up along the path, careful not to irritate the lazy, sated wasps. She replaces the lipstick, then retreats from view.

Unnoticed, I pull down the blinds, and with one wave of my hand the world is extinguished, leaching my senses of colour and time, and in the pastel greyness I allow myself to cry. Sudden tears blur my vision for just a moment, and then I blink them away. I once read a book, a self-help book I'd ordered on the Internet that had offered this advice: 'Cry only for a minute. Then, just breathe.' So I lie here just breathing. I hear Mary calling from her kitchen door, 'Cha-r-lie!' I hear the brittle cat biscuits rattling in their dish and I picture the semi-colon rising from his warm patch, now a startled question mark running home, a dash of tortoise-shell hastened by the frantic tinkling bell that dangles from his glittery collar.

Last year had been a record year for wasps, and as I recall, they'd strafed the soft fruits in all the gardens of the neighbourhood, placing bullet holes in almost every piece. It had been a slow summer, dragging on with relentless monotony. The late afternoons seemed to linger a little too long, gurgling like a soup pan left unregarded on the stove. Simmering, simmering, simmering ... I thought it was never going to end. I would watch Boris, my gardener, from the comfort of my window seat, my bare feet resting on a pile of National Geographics I'd been meaning to read. An electric fan set on low kept the air stirring, like a giant wooden spoon. Boris would wheel the barrow up the cobbled path, his thin naked shoulders jerking as he tipped a load of leaves and branches and grass cuttings onto the sweating compost heap, then he'd turn and make a thumbs up sign to me as I tried to busy myself at the window, with a book or sewing-scissors and cloth.

Boris was Albanian, his broken English both hobbled and strange. Each week I would leave a note, written simply in large print, with a list of jobs for him to do, tucking it into the moss lining of the hanging basket by the back door. Halfway through his allotted working hours, I'd place a cup of sweet black tea on a plastic tray and a shortbread biscuit or a slice of pie alongside it, sliding it out onto the porch. He knew to lift the tray, to find his wages secreted there; two ten pound notes pressed together in a Manila envelope, which he would empty and replace for use the following week. I didn't ask him how he lived, or where, but I had a feeling his was a rough world. He had the look of someone who was always on the run.

Boris had never set foot past my front door, had never questioned why. I felt a normality with him that had eluded me for many years. Friends had long since stopped calling by. At first they made conscious telephone calls, concealing their concern in a mundane repertoire. 'As long as you're sure you're okay,' they'd say. I could sense their exhalations, even before they'd hung up. It's hard to explain something alien, so I let them slip away, quietly.

The doorbell rings. Looking through the spy-hole I see Mary. She brings my weekly shopping round. I take a string of plastic bags from her, and write out a cheque. 'Fifty will do it,' she says, wiping her hands down the front of her apron. She knows not to stay.

Boris doesn't show today. When I pop my head around

the door to check, the note is still secured with a potting stake. The afternoon passes in a waiting game. Maybe he'll come, still. Maybe he won't. I boil the kettle, as usual, at three. I play back the answer-phone in case I've missed a message. When I return to my chair, the grass looks longer now, an unkempt beard of a lawn, onto which the pears have rolled, lying still like prey. I miss the sight of him, busy in the garden. I miss the bucket of flowers and pears he leaves for me - a pyramid of pears, the unspoiled ones, a simple offering by the boot scraper. In every season he finds something. Holly sprigs at Christmas, daffodils in April, peapods in July. He brings the garden to me, wrapped in sheets of newspaper or packed in pots. In the very corners of the rooms of my house, stemmed roses and sweetpeas sprout from old bottles and jam jars, and in the kitchen a vegetable patch of parsnip and radish, basil and lambs tongue spring from the shelves of my fridge. The pears though, are the only fruits. Large and plump, with pale golden-green skin, they are creamy, buttery and sweet. In the pear season, when they're plentiful, I sometimes poach them in honey and wine, and eat them at my table for one, as the sun slides away behind the rooftops.

As if to draw him here, I open the door, wide. I step back from the brightness, back away from the sound. I stand here, and just breathe. I breathe in and out, and in again. I watch an airplane climb into the stratosphere, a white trail unfurls in its wake. I picture the passengers, leaning back in submission, their seatbelts fastened uneasily over nervous knees. I see the cocky ones, unafraid to fly. I feel them swallow hard despite their brave conceit. I envy them their freedom, as I slide my toes across the floor, and hooking them around the bottom of the frame, I quietly, but surely, shut the door. The house is hushed but for the incessant humming-madman of the fridge, and the sound of me. My rhythmic footfall on the rugs and tiles. The clatter of utensils as I prepare an omelette on the stove. My sighs. And then, the phone rings.

'Hello,' I say.

' ... help me.'

'Sorry?'

'Please ... '

'I can't hear you very well,' I say, holding the handset tight to my ear as though it were a conch shell and the voice a distant rushing shore.

'Ple-ase, help me.'

'Who is this?' The line dies. The hissing is extinguished. 'Who is this?' I say again, peering into the mouthpiece at the silence there.

Shaken in part by the melodrama, partly by the interruption of routine, I replace the phone and watch it for a while. I dial 1471, but the caller has withheld. Who needs my help? Who needs me? The telephone remains hunched in the corner of the room, still and obsolete. I scrape away the remains of my supper, an oily glob hits the side of the bin, creeping floorwards like an escapee garden slug. I hadn't recognised the voice. Perhaps it had been a prank. Perhaps I wasn't needed after all - a fact I didn't linger on for long - it's hard to hear a plea for help, without in some way feeling strong, and the greater part of me had missed the buzz a sense of meaning gave to life.

Half-expecting the phone to ring again I climb, unhurriedly, upstairs to bed. Even if I notified the police, they would have nothing to go on. And they might have summoned me to the station. That would be unthinkable.

Despite the irritations of the day, I can feel myself vanishing, erased by sleep. It's the only time I allow myself to dream, yet as I'm drifting, something wakes me. My reading light is out and the window still ajar. A cold draught has probed the room with morgue-like fingers. Stumbling across the floor barefoot, I feel something wet beneath my toes. In the half-light it looks dark, like ink, spreading outwards, like a desperate hand. As I reach for the light switch, I hear the damp rasp of a cough, and then the voice.

'Do not be scared ... '

'Who is that?' I ask - all my fear lost to confusion.

'Borisav Yankovic,' it says.

'Boris?' I feel my way through the room towards the voice; Boris made indiscernible by the darkness. He is slumped against the wall, his hands clasped to his chest. His breaths are fast and shallow, like a secret-teller.

'What happened?' I ask, instinctively placing my palm upon his brow. Boris leans forward as if to answer then winces, crying out - a pained animal-like moan.

'I will call for an ambulance,' I say.

His hand grabs my wrist. 'No!' he says. 'No.'

'But you're hurt. You need help.'

'No ... please,' his eyes are the eyes of a boy.

'Here, hold on to me.' I slide one hand around his back, and tuck the other through his arm. With the little strength he has he grips me, and we do a strange disjointed tango to the bed.

In the bathroom, running water from the cold tap splashes over the side of the sink and hits the tiles, as I soak an old cloth and wring it out. Boris lies in embryonic submission on the crimson quilt. As I sit beside him, he curls up tight as a bud, hugging his sides. 'Let me see' I say to him, gently pushing away his hands and lifting his blood-stained T- shirt, to reveal a deep gash slashed across his rib cage. Applying pressure with the damp cloth, the blood flow stems. The coolness and, I imagine, my presence, calms him.

Rummaging in the bathroom cabinet, I find gauze and cotton wadding and a roll of paper tape, with which I make a dressing for his wound.

'Tell me how this happened,' I say softly. But Boris is gone, finding relief in a deep unconsciousness, the story of how this came to be, resting for now, silently within his slumbering form. As I drape a blanket over him, tucking it around him, like a pastry lid, careful not to wake him, I notice something sticking out from within the breast pocket of his denim jacket. Fearing that it may be a weapon, I fetch a pair of gloves from the wardrobe, and put them on before I remove it, deftly, slowly. Boris sleeps on, his breaths regular now, his fists unfurled, so that his fingers are both resting yet readying themselves, like new green shoots after the last frost.

In my gloved hands, I hold a small bundle, wrapped and

tied with string. Deceptively small, it weighs heavy in my palm. Boris stirs. Waiting until he settles again, I unwrap the object, turning it over in my hand, holding it to the light. From within the leather folder, several objects slide. They're mostly papers. I spread them out over the bed, a mosaic of newspaper clippings, photographs and letters, handwritten in navy ink. I cannot read the foreign script, but no matter, what is lost in language is understood in pictures. It is all there. Screaming. An open grave. Young men in civilian clothes, machine guns slung across their shoulders, slouching, looking on. Villagers, male relatives of the victims perhaps, stunned and scared, their hands pushed firmly into their trouser pockets, their wide eyes staring into the news cameras for answers. Old women, their black headscarves pulled tight around their gaping jaws, sunk to their knees, wailing, their knotted hands raised to the sky, presumably to God.

In one photograph, which was wrapped with a sort of desolate reverence in crinkled sheets of tissue, a family is standing together on the slatted porch of a rustic farmhouse. The elder is wearing a piliz, a felt hat, his peasant-like clothes tired and tattered, his whole face a smile. Robust pride directed at the camera lens. In the foreground, is a small boy;

he holds out a stick, a switch of willow, waving it towards a clutch of pepper-feathered hens that seem to scurry from the orchard, which stands to the side of the house. Fruit trees. Pears perhaps. I wonder about the boy, how old he might have been. At the time of the Kosovo-Serbian massacres, Boris must have been a child.

I fold the keepsakes back into the bundle and place it on the bedside. I know now how he had come to be here, and why he had refused medical attention. An illegal immigrant, a refugee, displaced, alone, Boris sought sanctuary, now, in the shelter of my home. When death is known, when it lives in you daily, it is hard not to recognize in others the commonality it brings, and in that, to know them too. And in the presence of his story, my own fears fade.

Inspiration is a seed planted. It is morning now. With a tray of black tea and triangles of buttered toast, in one hand, I lift the blinds. Boris is a starfish on the bed. The dappled beams of light move upon his face, causing him to stir, as though they're nudging him awake. Outside, the sky is streaked with pink and purple ribbons. Mary walks to the bird table and scrapes off her cutting board with the edge of a knife. She sees me at the window, and waves. I wave back. I wonder if she knows. I wonder if, in the dark nights of quiet homes, she suspects a drama such as this.

As the mid-day sun ascends, dragging the unstoppable hours of my life with it to the mocha clouds, I am compelled to act, to overcome the fear that has held me here. To somehow honour the very freedom this paradox affords. I have tried many times, but this time ... this time, things are different. I am a field of flowers, unfolding, reaching for the light. I tread lightly down the stairs. The door opens and I am Dorothy in The Wizard of Oz. All the colours in the garden intensify, even as I watch them glow. Suddenly, everything seems too bright for my senses, too loud. Lupin and feverfew bound from the soil, and towering over Mary's hedgerow, sombre trees stand motionless, their limp leaves wilting just a little, thirsting for rain. In the long grass, the pears are turning to pulp under the heavy sun. The only movements are the incessant flies, cruising on the zephyr, too stupid to rest, and the black crows shifting about, flapping the dander from their hot wings.

I breathe the garden in, as though it were strength itself, as though the plants held in their roots a potion that could carry me afar. I close my eyes, and holding on to the doorframe, I place one foot outside. I am ten years old again, dipping my toes into the sea, daring to feel the waves around my ankles, pressing my heels into the sand and the many broken shells that scrunch and crackle beneath my soft-soled feet. I stay like that awhile, and then, let go. I take a step. I feel the air swoop around my legs, bathing me. I feel the heat of the sun warm my scalp.

All the sounds of summer radiate from the many gardens, and the winding streets and the play park and the flag-blue sky.

And I'm alright.

Kneeling onto the long blades of softly growing grass, as though in prayer, I place a mound of ripe pears in the folds of my cotton skirt, inhaling, not merely breathing, as if for the very first time.

I spend the day baking pies and freezing them. In the evening, as the garden cools, I place a dish of peeled pears into the oven. A caramelised infusion of maple, cinnamon and fragrant pear juice fills the kitchen. Plumes of rich steam waft into the hallway and ascend the staircase. I lay the table and turn down the lights. I pour myself a cup of tea, and sip it by the window. Mary is unpegging a row of washing from the line, arms and legs flap at her, embracing her, as a gust of wind rolls over the hedgerows. Charlie watches her, unblinking, from the shelter of a deckchair. The sky darkens, and from somewhere far off in the distance a rumble of thunder sends Mary rushing to her backdoor, leaving one last sock dangling in surrender to the approaching storm.

'Excuse me ... ' I turn around and see Boris standing in my kitchen. 'Please ... ' he gestures towards the table.

'Yes, yes of course,' I say, pulling up a chair for him. Boris moves slowly. He sits down, cautiously. Surveying the garden through the dusk he blows across the surface of his tea. 'I am sorry,' he says, 'the grass ... it is ... '

'Boris, please, not to worry,' I say, smiling at his sincerity. 'Now, tell me, do you like pears?'

The Tea Party

Anne Ponsonby

Julie opened the oven door and took out a tray of scones. Light as air and fluffy as a feather duvet, she put them to cool. Beside them lay rows of brownies like soldiers standing to attention.

Julie was a pretty, youngish, plumpish widow. Jim had died at forty-five from a heart attack possibly due, in part, to her cooking. She had thrown herself into making extra money from her expertise in the kitchen, keeping herself busy and as cheerful as possible.

The kettle had just boiled when in marched her next door neighbour, Nicola ('Don't EVER call me Nicky'). Everything about Nicola shone from her liquorice coloured hair to her 'high as the Empire State Building' black patent stilettos. Her heels clicked across the kitchen floor and she sat down carefully so as to keep her black business suit uncreased.

She waved away the scones and the brownies accepting a cup of tea, black, no sugar. She rarely ate anything but occasionally grazed on a carrot or two. Her fridge was full of mineral water and she was Managing Partner of a major accountancy firm in the nearby town.

They were good friends and when she gave her elegant dinner parties she didn't let on that Julie had cooked every dish. She merely shrugged when receiving compliments on her food and intimated that she had just thrown them together between important emails and text messages.

She offered Julie good advice on how to handle a small income. Julie's dream was to open an old fashioned tea shop selling proper home baked food. She would call it Julie's Comfort Corner. All she needed was a rich investor.

'So, how are things?' she asked, munching on a scone loaded with butter and jam.

'Well, you know that conference I told you about? It is now firmly fixed and on Saturday week, fifteen are coming for the Seminar. Japanese, Indians, Hong Kong Chinese and … some Americans. I am really worrying about what to do with them on Saturday. They arrive first thing and are sure to be feeling jet lagged. Dinner will be too late, lunch too early, what shall I do? I want to impress them with something British. Trouble is they have done everything, and been everywhere, and unless they have Marco Pierre White in the kitchen they feel short-changed.'

Julie thought for a few minutes. She had recently been taken to tea at the Ritz by her godmother. This had been booked four weeks in advance and was a mere £40 a head. It had been delicious.

'Tell you what, let's give them a proper British tea party. We can invite them at five o'clock. I'll guarantee some wonderful food, what do you think?'

Julie was surprised that Nicola liked the idea. She left saying she would like the menu ASAP and went home murmuring, 'Waitresses in frilly aprons and a butler to open the door.'

The next two weeks flew by as Julie thought and re-thought the menus. A butler and two waitresses were booked. Flowers were ordered and a cleaning firm booked to clean an already immaculate flat. Nicola worked away at her clever accountancy ideas and decided that she would wear slinky black as opposed to business black and spent all Friday at the beauty salon.

Julie washed her hair and tied it back with a ribbon. Her new apron with smiley faces all over it was ready. Many hours had been spent planning the perfect tea party.

On Saturday she arrived early with all the food. She had made miniature sandwiches, smoked salmon, crab and watercress, cucumber and cream cheese, her special light and mouth-watering chicken liver pate. She planned to bake her scones at the last minute. These would be covered in whipped Cornish cream and her home-made strawberry jam, with wild strawberries. The cakes small, medium and huge were ready. A light as air Victoria sponge, a dark and glossy chocolate, a lemon drizzle, plus a tray of cupcakes decorated with the national flags of all the guests. The centrepiece was a spectacular Croque-en-Bouche normally only served at French weddings. Tiny little choux pastry balls filled with cream and arranged in a tall pyramid. It looked amazing, covered with golden spun sugar and almost too pretty to demolish.

The tables were covered with glistening white damask tablecloths; the waitresses stood smiling, their aprons frilled and frothed, showing their teeth (as instructed by Nicola) and the butler stood to attention waiting for the doorbell to ring. Nicola looked elegant in a floor length black silk jersey dress. She was a perfect picture. Julie stood in the background and felt herself relaxing. She had never produced such ambrosial food.

The doorbell rang and the guests arrived. The Japanese bowed, the Hong Kong Chinese looked around mentally pricing everything in the room. The Indians saw the tables ready for tea, remembered their links with the British, smiled and hoped for cucumber sandwiches. The Americans had never seen anything like it.

The champagne sparkled, conversation flowed and Nicola was a truly professional Hostess. After half an hour the Butler stepped forward and said, 'Madam, tea is served.' There was a rush towards the tea tables. The guests piled their plates high and went and sat in little groups. Nicola came and went distributing her special brand of charm. Julie saw her food disappear and guests returning for more.

Conversation was mainly about financial investments. One of the Americans – Joe Daley - asked Nicola who had organised the amazing tea party and for once she didn't pretend she had done it all herself. Julie was introduced, everyone clapped and Joe Daley asked for her phone number. He was planning to update his chain of American coffee shops. Could tea become the new coffee? Would he invite Julie to be his consultant? Could he persuade his compatriots to forget the Boston Tea Party and welcome the British back?

A year later a sign spelling 'Julie's Comfort Corner' stood above a spanking new teashop. It was rapidly becoming successful. The clients included 'Ladies Who Used To Lunch' but now booked tables for 'Special Teas'. Joe had invested in her expertise and she had made several trips to America to help him decide on locations, menus, advertising and franchising. They had become firm friends and one dream had come true. She remembered thinking the longer it took for a dream to manifest itself, the more likely it was to happen.

Oedipus, Shmoedipus ...
Jenny McRobert

My Sigmund is famous and I love him to bits, but I have to admit that sometimes he gets on my nerves, with his 'phallic this and his phallic that.'

I say, 'Sigmund, I hardly even noticed your father's penis, let alone envied it. Carry on like this and you'll turn into a dirty old man one day, you mark my words.'

So, I'm on my way into town when I meet Mrs Levy, you know, the one with the husband who's such a looker, those shoulders ... oy, if I were only twenty years younger.

I say, 'Mrs Levy, you look like a princess, so glowing and healthy.' She's on the plain side mind you.

She says to me, 'Mrs Freud, your Sigmund is wonderful; he cured me of my terrible fear of spiders ... I feel so free!'

Feh, she always was a drama queen. I make all the right noises but put it down to great sex with that husband ... and chicken soup. My recipe, of course.

So, I am about to put a second helping on his plate.

I say, 'Sigmund you're not eating, you're getting so *thin*. Don't you like my knedles any more? Why do you have to chomp on those *filthy* cigars all day and night?'

He just sighs and puts on that 'face', the one that people call 'tortured and interesting.' Personally, I think it's his piles playing up again.

Now, I am a very understanding person and there is nothing that Sigmund likes better than analysing a good dream or two. So I think, I'll cheer him up with one of mine.

I say, 'Sigmund, last night I dreamed I was flying ... just like a bird over the hill tops, darting in out of buildings, flapping away, up, up, up.' Perhaps I overdid it a teensy bit.

But he perks up and says, 'Interesting, we'll free associate' and when he says, 'Llama', I obligingly say, 'Banana.'

Well, he goes on about dreams and sex and all that phallic stuff again, blah, blah, blah. Personally I put it down to the gherkins I had with my dinner last night.

So, what can I do? I try to understand. I know, to many people, he's a big man, but he won't eat properly, or wear his scarf when it's windy. And I've never seen him in those gloves I knitted him last Hanukkah ... and does he call me? No.

Oedipus, Shmoedipus, what does it matter? As long a boy loves his mother.

Village Competition
Claudia Pettifer

Lucy James hastily put her fruitcake in her oven, and wiped her hands on a pink-spotted Cath Kidston tea towel.

'Mummy, Ethan knocked over my tower,' a yelp came from the playroom.

'Come on you two, play nicely for another 10 minutes and you can watch CBeebies.'

Lucy put the kettle on, switched the oven timer on and twisted her hair back into a large clip. Entering the WI Christmas cake competition had seemed a good idea at the time; all part of living the dream that she and Tom had when they had bought Robin Cottage to renovate. Shame she hadn't factored in the kitchen being stripped bare and her complete lack of culinary experience. It probably wasn't the best time to make her first ever fruit cake but she had complete faith in Nigella.

A mile or so down Green Lane, in the large kitchen at White Lodge, Penny Granger was unwrapping her delivery from Fortnum's. The cake smelled wonderful. She did feel a tad guilty cheating for the second year in a row, but between the horses, the dogs and lastly and least, Hugo, her stockbroker husband, she had no time for cooking. Anyway, she mused, it'll be interesting to see if Fortnum's achieves a higher position than last year's offering from Harrods, which had only come third.

'Come on boys' she slapped her thigh and reached for her muddy wellies and dog leads. Her two red setters bounded towards her, immediately recognising the signs. Penny lovingly stroked each dog's silky ears. What with Hugo's increasingly frequent sojourns to town and twins Toby and Seb's departure to uni, these two were her most loyal companions.

Letty Lovejoy placed her bicycle against the railings of Honeysuckle Cottage. Out of the capacious wicker basket she delivered some eggs, carefully wrapped, to prevent any breakages on the ride from Longdown Farm. The bike had served her well as district midwife and now kept her fit and mobile in her retirement. The eggs were still warm and she reckoned on them being one of the key ingredients which explained her five year reign as Worthy Bottom Christmas Cake Champion.

Inside her neat, ordered kitchen all the remaining ingredients were neatly weighed out in bowls as she set about creating this year's triumphant offering.

'Well there's no point in changing perfection, Mrs C.,' she announced to her faithful moggy, confident that this year she would again be victorious.

The Laurels was a modern cul-de-sac on the edge of the village. At number 5 Delia Sinclair admired her cake over a china cup of Earl Grey tea. The house may be small, she told her friends, but it was so practical. She and Derek had become resigned to the fact that there weren't to be any little Sinclairs, some years ago, and at that time Delia took up the position of Doctor's receptionist at the small village practice, a great job for the village busybody.

Poor Delia was one of those people who always had a chip on her shoulder and found it hard to accept the success of those around her. It was for this reason she was determined to win this year's WI completion and show Letty Lovejoy that she wasn't the only person around who could bake a cake. Sadly for Delia, she wasn't one of those who could. It was for this reason Delia had asked her younger sister, Hazel, if she could possibly bake a cake for the church bazaar. Well it was sort of true. Any way Hazel with her three children and four bed detached and her talent as a cook, sort of owed it to her sister, didn't she? Well that's how Delia saw it.

Village Competition - Claudia Pettifer

Two weeks later outside the village hall, locals were beginning to congregate. Letty had arrived in good time to help set up. Delia's Toyota Yaris was dwarfed by Penny's Range Rover. Lucy, running late as ever, rolled in at the last minute, parking her old Volvo estate at a rather jaunty angle. She unpacked herself, the kids and the cake and all of a fluster she bundled into the hall.

This year the judges were, as always, Lawrence Wilson, the vicar, Freda, his wife and the WI president, Brenda Saunders. Theirs was the power to decide who made the best jam, who knitted the most creative creature and who made the moistest, most flavoursome Christmas cake.

By about two o'clock it was cake-judging time and all three, with earnest expressions and clasping clipboards took a small piece of each cake. First up was Delia Sinclair's (sister's) cake.

'Well, this is delicious Delia, Brenda enthused with her mouth full.

'Mmmm frightfully moist,' commented the vicar.

'Nonsense Lawrence, it's rather dry and a little too nutty in my view,' Freda retorted.

'Yes of course, dear,' Lawrence hastily agreed as they moved on to cake number two; Penny's purchase from Fortnum's.

'Well I must say this really has an exquisite flavour,' said Brenda. 'Funny I never had Penny down as a cook, but this really is rather yummy. What do you think Vicar?'

'Err, what do you reckon darling, do we like this one?' He looked humbly at Freda.

'Hmmm, it does have a certain something,' Freda savoured her mouthful.

'Mmmm. What is it?'

'Brandy,' smiled Lawrence.

The next cake was Letty's. She was confidently presiding over the tasting.

'Ah, Letty dear, I'm sure this will be excellent; your usual recipe?' Brenda enquired.

'Naturally,' beamed Letty.

The judges each took a mouthful of the cake, and then another.

'Ooh Letty, it's definitely up to your usual standard.'

Letty beamed.

Village Competition – Claudia Pettifer

'Ah! Last but not least, Lucy James.' Brenda looked at the little nametag in front of the last cake. 'I'm not sure I recognise that name.'

She looked around but, at that moment Lucy was taking Joe to the loo while Ethan banged on the cubicle door.

'She's new to the village, she and her husband are doing up Robin Cottage. They've two monstrous little boys.'

'Freda, that's a little harsh, I'm sure the boys just wanted to join in the Nativity Play at the crib service. They didn't mean to knock over the manger.'

'Yes well, that's as maybe, but the howling Mary made and the ensuing fight really did spoil things for everyone.' Freda said while taking a mouthful of Lucy's cake.

'I'll tell you something though, this cake is absolutely delicious. Brenda, thoughts?'

'Gosh you're right Freda.' Brenda looked a little worried as she marked the cake.

Half an hour later it was results time and the murmurs of anticipation hushed as Brenda took to the small wooden stage. The four cake contestants impatiently stood through the jam, shortbread and knitting results. Lucy's boys were really starting to play up big time.

Village Competition – Claudia Pettifer

'Come on boys, just a mo. Mummy wants to see if they liked her cake. I'll get you a Happy Meal if I win. (Fat chance.)' Lucy muttered under her breath as with one voice the two boys started to chant.

'Mummy, Mummy, Mummy!'

Eyes turned to Lucy who, with crimson face looked to the ground.

'And the winner of this year's Christmas fruit cake competition with an outstanding score of 18 out of 20 is ... Lucy James. Well done Lucy.'

Brenda made her announcement and again all eyes turned to Lucy. She blushed with pride. Then, as she looked round the room, was a little alarmed to see the hostility looking back at her.

That evening after the mayhem of bath time, in the half plastered living room, Lucy felt a little uneasy that maybe village life wasn't all it was cracked up to be.

A Not So Vintage Tale
Angela Ramsell

Julia looked surprised when Ernst got down on blended knee.

'I can't believe that you have the gallo to ask me what I think you are going to ask!'

Ernst's face went a deep full-bodied red whilst Julia's was rather blush. Chardonnay who was standing outside the open window listening went white.

Ernst stood up and walked over to the cabernet looking despondent. Julia leaned against the columbard with a disappointed look on her face. She had no idea that he would lose his bottle or she wouldn't have said anything. They looked at one another, each wondering what the other was thinking.

Julia sat down with a plonk on the leather sofa and sat there fingering the vine in the pot next to her wondering what she could do to encourage him to carry on with his question.

'Don't lose heart Ernst. Can't we just cork about it?'

At this point the french door flew open and Chardonnay entered the room shaking the rain off her barolla.

'Has he asti you yet?' she said to Julia with a little grenache.

'The brut! I can't believe that he told you what he was going to do? You of all people. How could he do that to me?' Julia said reisling from the sofa.

'Julia, don't get in a tempranillo over it. He'd had a couple of drinks and was feeling nervous. He wanted to shiraz feelings about you with someone.'

'But not you, his little prosecco! Why couldn't he have shared his feelings with Piper Heidsieck, his friend of many years. Many's the evening they both went to clubs for a bit of rioja and roll.'

Ernst listening to this turned blanc de blancs and felt quite malbec. His stomach felt a little bubbly and he left the room as quickly as a champagne cork leaving a bottle.

When he got outside the room everything went pinot noir. He fell to the ground hitting his head on the large zinfandel of the ancient trunk in the hall.

'What was that noise?' Julia asked Chardonnay.

They both rushed out of the room and found Ernst laying in a spreading pool of bull's blood. Julia bent down and felt for his pulse. 'He's dead! I chianti believe it. The love of my life. Now we will never be known as Ernst and Julia Gallo. The world of wine will never be the semillon.

Cooking up some Office Gossip
(aka Food for Thought)
Carole Hastings

'Now that his Belle Helene has gone, it's made Mr Barkham Blue. He's really cut up.'

'I know he really crumbled the day she left. I always thought she was a bit of a tart. Trottering about on her Stiltons, not giving Two Hoots about the skate of the filo – it looks a proper Eton Mess. Always trifling with John Dorey's affections too.'

'Rosemary caught her making ice at that sweet Basil from marketing – she was giving him some big quiches at her leaving do – too steamy for my liking.'

'By Eccles cake, he could devil my kidneys any day!'

'Naah – he's steaming drunk every Fry-day. Lives in a semi freddo but carries on like he's lard of the manor. Eel think he's souper – mincing about in that Black Bomber jacket.'

'Well they make a juicier pear than her and Barkham – he's a right Tunworth. Always wining and I've never heard him truckle in all the thyme I've been here.'

'Who do you think will get her roll? Apparently she earned a mint. I Knorr she got a roasting for leeking how much.'

'I think he'll try and poach that nice Sole Veronique – she seems like a good sauté.'

Really? That old trout Olive's set her carp at it. She'll be simmering if she's pastried over again.'

'That's all berry well but she's difficult to pudding up with. Always grilling her staff about their apple turnover figures and getting them in a stew for no raisin.'

'Mmm, you're probably right, Veronique's a peach and knows her onions, so it looks like she'll get her just dessert.'

Written in Stone

In a place far away, in a cave, in a hollow, in a rock, in a stone, between layers of sediment, there's a creature that's seen the beginning of time. It is curled in a ball very small; it is old and it holds many secrets but it won't talk to me.

Perhaps I'll look it up on the web, to see what the experts have said? Or I'll write to a scientist, who'll come and unfurl its many mannerisms and mysteries to me. How did it live? What did it eat? Are there are still relatives around we can meet?

I want to know about its journey through time, but the creature I've found is encased in the ground, and they'd break all the stones to remove it, or they'd cordon it off to protect the delicate spines when they trample around to exhume it. I want it to stay, so perhaps I'll walk on in the dark of the day...

I stand near the primordial brink to linger, to ponder and think; and then I decide I'll do something daring, because finding this creature that nobody knows, is not half as much fun without sharing. I tell Anya, Catherine and Ben, about the creature that'd turned into ore. And soon we embark to a tomb in the dark, where the body had frozen one perilous night and look round in the beam of an LED light.

The creature that once swam in the slime had become a petrified prisoner in a castle of lime. An ammonite spiralled and gracious; that had waited for us to discover her fate since at least before the Cretaceous.

Together, in the cave, in the hollow, in the rock, between layers of sediment, we found the ammonite's story written in stone, a geological crime discovered by Anya, Catherine, Ben, and I as we travelled for millions of years back in time.

Hilary Gregory

The River

Madeleine Woosnam

When I look back it seems I began with the river. Most likely I will end there too, though the end will be a while in coming and anything is possible before then.

Some of my earliest memories are of the river. The cold that made me squeal as it poured in over the top of my wellingtons when I had taken that one step too far. And the squelching all the way home. The calm of a summer's day with the river slipping silently past and winking as it went. The fear, when I fell in and was sure that I would drown as I was swept downstream, my waders filling as I went and clutching onto my precious rod for all I was worth. Until the river took me in his arms and delivered me safely to his shores.

The time when I hadn't visited the river for a while, so he came to visit me. Stealing up the garden path and floating the rush mat in the downstairs lavatory. I took care after that not to neglect my friend. I didn't want him visiting again. Sometimes I heard him roaring in the night as though in pain, full of red, Welsh mud so that he looked like a river of blood surging through the sodden countryside taking everything in his way. And I would wake to hear him calling into my dreams until my head was full of the sound of him.

Once he collected a whole field full of hay bales, just for a laugh, and I saw them bobbing and weaving, congratulating themselves on their escape, as they hurried towards the sea. Often I saw whole trees rushing downstream, bent on destruction. And sometimes the pathetic body of a dead sheep swept away in the raging torrent and left hanging out to dry on a branch as the waters receded. Oh yes, I know the river in all his moods. The way he can change in an instant and sometimes when you least expect it. The river is my friend and companion. He knows all my hopes and fears. My secrets and dreams. For I told them all to him. From start to finish. Beginning to end. I will begin, and end, with the river.

Salut d'Amour

(Love's Greeting)

To 'Carice', Park Road, Westgate,
We clattered up the street,
To lunch with Gran and Grandad,
This really was a treat.

'You mind the paintwork,' Gran yelled,
As we slid along the floor,
To sniff lunch bubbling on the stove,
And hide behind the door.

The leathery scent of Grandad
From cobbling boot and shoe,
Reached us. 'He's here,' we cried
And sprung out shouting, 'Boo.'

Soon the steak and kidney pud
Was turned out on a plate.
As Gran sliced through the crust,
We began to salivate.

Lunch done, Gran lit the single fag
She allowed herself each day,
Whilst Grandad tuned his fiddle up,
And then began to play.

'Salut d'Amour, á Carice',
Warbled through the room.
The two of them had named their house
From this, their favourite tune.

And now I grasp their love's exchange,
As his bow kissed those strings:
Her cooking kept him down to earth,
His music gave her wings.

Maria Watson

A Small Man

Soft candlelight brings in the Sabbath with a blessing
Prayers read from right to left
We are reprieved for a while from bed
He is silent
Nothing said, nothing heard
Impassive face, though brown eyes flame-flicker
Above his neat moustache

Rubbing our eyes, we laugh
As Nana tells one of her many stories
Expressive round pink arms
Thick silver hair
Sealed in silent mines like Quasimodo
He does not hear her lively chimes

I do not know of the sad childhood
Punctuated by blows and boxed ears
Made to sleep on workshop rags
Punished by a father who wanted
A tall son
Grandpa became a Savile Row tailor
Proud, skilled, respected

A Small Man – Jenny McRobert

Sitting behind a newspaper

His retreat from our organised mayhem

He is an enigma to me

But somehow he draws me to him

I, on the floor by his feet, content to sit

At Grandpa's temple

For an instant a warm flash

From deep brown eyes

His wide smile

Breaking over me like sunlight

I wish I could reach into his mind

And heal his pain

That he might hear pattering

The warm soft rain

Of my love

Jenny McRobert

The Journey
Peggie Keeley

I suppose it was a comparatively short journey but at the time it seemed like a hundred miles.

It started in the early evening as we travelled from the seaside town, across Portsdown Hill and on to the road to Petersfield. There was very little traffic and vehicles were going slowly, the half covered lights not making it any easier. By the time we reached the Midhurst road it was getting dark. I was feeling very scared and still couldn't understand why I was being taken away from my home. The journey continued along country roads as strange shapes loomed up in the dimmed light from the car. On reaching Cowdray we drove very carefully to avoid the deer in the park but finally reached our destination - my new home at Rectory Cottage with my Aunt and Uncle.

We had come to the end of the journey. It was Friday 1st September 1939.

War was declared two days later.

Two Biscuits and a Gas Mask
Marjorie Andrews

Sitting in my lap are two biscuits and a gas mask. Bewildered as to what is happening, I smile at my mother through the train window. She has my sister in her arms; a baby of two. No emotion shows on her face. I don't understand. Don't even remember a hug before I climbed aboard this huge black monster, belching smoke and steam.

Nothing makes sense. Nobody tells me anything about what is going to happen. My teacher sits opposite in this place with itchy seats. No smiles, no conversation, just a nod in acknowledgment that I exist. She speaks to another person, who I do not recognise. I now know, after seventy-two years, it was a person in authority for the evacuation of children from Manchester in 1939.

I can remember worrying about how I was going to have a wee. Always uppermost in my mind when going somewhere new - how to get to a lavatory.

This is my story as an evacuee and the memory is still as painful today as it was then. Nightmares happen, out of the blue, for no reason, of that traumatic time in my childhood.

I have recollections of being in an old hall, tired,

hungry with another little girl of my age. Her name was Cynthia and we were in the same class at school. It was getting dark and the concern in our teacher's voice made me feel insecure.

'Somebody has to take them.'

'You will have to go back up the road and try with some of the refusals and prick their conscience.'

I remember them knocking on the door of a house with coloured windows. A woman with grey hair scraped back off her forehead opened it.

'I said no and I mean no. I do not want a filthy child from the slums of Manchester.'

'It's six o'clock, she hasn't had a proper meal all day and she should be going to bed.'

'It seems I have no option.'

The teacher walked away; the beautiful coloured glass door closed behind me.

She walked me into a small room with a tiled grate. There was a table in the middle and a door open showing a small kitchen beyond. It looked cosy and inviting. This was my world for the next nine months and the bed I slept in at the top of the stairs.

She fed me and kept me clean. She never spoke to me

other than to tell me to eat and go to bed. On reflection, I remember there were three more people in the house; a daughter named Ena, who must have been about ten years of age, a husband, and a grown up son who I only remember being aware of when I heard him say goodbye to the family.

One Sunday afternoon the daughter invited me into the parlour to look at her piano. I think she must have been lonely as no other children ever came to play. Her mother would be out all day at Church and wasn't expected home until teatime. The parlour, a hallowed sanctuary, it seemed like heaven.

Heaven that night it was not. Terrible sobs came from I know not where.

'Won't do it again Mummy!'

'Please, please forgive me.'

Only words from Dad.

'Don't be so hard on the child.'

That was it.

Never, never again did I go anywhere in that house other than sit at the top of the cellar steps where I played with my coloured pegboard and read my Enid Blyton stories. To this day they are still my favourite, especially 'The Magic Faraway Tree' and the 'Magic Wishing Chair'.

The cursed small bedroom at the top of the stairs should have been my sanctuary but, because of the fear of bedwetting, it was a constant nightmare of guilt and the shame of the smell of a wet bed in the morning.

To give them their due, they did take me out once. It had been my birthday a few months before when they announced we were going out. I now know it was the Winter Gardens Blackpool, and the person I saw was Harry Hemsley, a ventriloquist. He used to sit by himself on a chair in the middle of the stage talking to imaginary children. Sitting there on the edge of my seat, I kept expecting them to appear on the stage but of course, they never did, much to my disappointment.

In the interval, they had coffee, with a chocolate biscuit. I had Oxo because I didn't know about coffee drinking. With the Oxo came a cream cracker. Plain and insipid and I could not understand why I couldn't have a chocolate biscuit. It's not done they said and that was it.

For my birthday my mother had sent me a one shilling and sixpenny postal order but until the trip to the theatre I had never been allowed to spend it. They said I could purchase a bar of my favourite Barker and Dobson's grapefruit chocolate but I was only to eat a small portion. I ate most of it and, to my horror, I was sick that night. Was it the joy of so much excitement in one go? I later learned she had written to my Mum saying I was a disgusting child.

The bedwetting continued so they took me to hospital to see if there was something wrong. It was just fear of the unknown and my surroundings.

She left me to go to school by myself, along a busy road, leading to the beach, which I never once went to the whole time I was evacuated. It was a make do and mend sort of school. A Nissan hut with all the kids bungled together of all ages. A lot of bullying went on from the older children. God bless my teacher, Miss Warrington, she took me to the local library and got me as many books as I could read. She was wonderful. I thought she had magic powers because her hair was white either side of her head and the rest was nearly black. Such a beautiful caring person.

Many children were bullied by the older children, including myself, by a very large lad called Raymond who used to live in the next street to me in Manchester. He was absolutely huge, but he grew into the most delightful young man. His father was a prisoner of war for almost five years, having been captured at Dunkirk. My father survived Dunkirk and didn't tell me his story until about a month before he died of cancer at the age of 70.

How did I survive each day? God only knows, but I did.

My Dad came home on leave and came to see me with my Mum. It was the only other visit I had. He took one look and said,

'Pack her bags'

I was going home.

The hug I gave him I can remember with clarity to this day. His scratchy Air Force Uniform. The smell of my Mum's scent, Grossmith's Phul Nana, which she used most of her life.

How we got back to Manchester I cannot remember but I do remember walking into my Aunt's house - we lived in the same street. As we went in through the back entry heard my Mum say,

'Now you are home behave yourself.'

I don't remember being naughty as a child. Perhaps its something she just had to say.

*

Seventy-two years have gone by.

It's the year of my Golden Wedding, the date, 17th June 2011. We are so lucky to have been married for fifty years and still enjoying each other's company.

We celebrated our anniversary with the family; daughter,

husband and two grandsons in the seaside town of Sidmouth, Devon. We stayed at The Victoria Hotel, which overlooked the sea, which was superb.

The town, a time warp straight out the thirties, old-fashioned, with small shops.

We visited the local museum, which housed the most wonderful collection of Honiton lace and stories of the folk who have lived in this special place.

My daughter and I had seen an old-fashioned perfume shop and decided to go back and leave the chaps in the Museum. As we entered there was a display - the biggest in the shop - advertising Grossmith's Phul Nana perfume. The price, one hundred and forty pounds for the smallest bottle.

How my Mum would have laughed. Perhaps she was just saying 'Hello' at this special time in my life.

Warm Beer and Spam Sandwiches
Anne Ponsonby

During the darkest days of World War II, an organisation was formed called Special Operations Executive. France may have been defeated but there were many brave men and women who were prepared to resist the Nazis.

Winston Churchill said to those in charge, 'Set Europe ablaze'. Agents were recruited, trained and parachuted into France by Lysander aircraft. Sometimes these aircraft landed in fields with only torchlight to guide them.

Among these agents were fifty-five women. They were trained to shoot and kill the enemy. Many of them were radio operators who sent and received messages by Morse Code. Nineteen of them were captured and perished at Ravensbruck or other concentration camps. Their names are remembered and every year there is a service at St Paul's, Knightsbridge to commemorate their bravery. Some were married with small children; some were working as shop assistants or in other jobs. They had to speak perfect French to be accepted for training. They were all volunteers.

There are many that are unknown to the public, but several have had their stories told in films or on television.

Odette Churchill was one who suffered torture but refused to give any information. Violette Szabo was another who also suffered torture and was eventually executed at Ravensbruck. Nancy Wake has just died in her nineties.

Every time they went on air, they were in danger as they were followed by radio detector vans, and if discovered faced being tortured, imprisoned or shot.

I was fifteen years old when World War II began and had to wait until I was eighteen before being allowed to join one of the women's services.

By chance I met someone who had just been accepted by the First Aid Nursing Yeomanry (the FANYs). She told me that she would probably learn how to drive and ferry senior army officers around the country. It didn't sound very exciting but I was desperate to join the war effort and even more desperate to escape from my mother who wanted me to stay at home.

I applied and was accepted. To my amazement I was then informed that I would be trained to be a wireless operator and expected to become proficient in learning the Morse Code in order to send and receive messages to the French Resistance.

This was definitely more exciting and for three months we listened to Morse for eight hours a day. It was essential that we reached high speeds in order to take down the messages quickly and accurately. After de-coding they were sent to head office for action. Head office was in a Marks and Spencer's building in Baker Street, which proved to be a very good cover.

After training we were posted to Grendon Underwood in Buckinghamshire, where we lived and worked on eight hour shifts, twenty-four hours a day. We had to listen for the message on fairly primitive radio sets. Patience was required as sometimes no messages came through and we wondered if the agents were in trouble as they sat with their radio sets, probably in an abandoned building or on top of a hill knowing that they were in mortal danger every time they went on air.

We were told that it was strictly forbidden to send any messages, using plain language. We were careful to obey this rule even though we were tempted to send a personal message to the operator we were listening to.

June 1st 1944 arrived and we were told that we could not leave our camp under any circumstances. We wondered why, but had no suspicion that preparations for D-Day were underway.

On June 6th I was sitting at my radio set listening for the call sign which would indicate there was a message waiting to be sent. To my amazement and excitement I suddenly realised I was taking down the message in French and in plain language.

'Vive la France, Vive la Grande Bretagne, Vive les Allies' this continued and I waved to the Sergeant in Charge who came over to see what was happening. When he saw the message, he grabbed it and literally ran to the office to telephone Head Office with the news that for one radio operator, in France, D-Day had begun.

I still get goose flesh when I remember that incident which gave me the knowledge that after so many years, the liberation of Europe had begun.

That evening we celebrated with warm beer and spam sandwiches.

I have always been proud to have been part of an organisation where there were so many incredibly brave men and women. In particular, the women who joined SOE as agents were among the first to face the enemy with a gun in their hands, knowing the danger that faced them.

Pond on Army Land

We went to walk on Army land,
where crickets clicked in silent sunshine
and I sat down by a pond where the yellow
flowered gorse spiked the soft sand and
grass peeped over layers of orange clay
gouged deep by spade cuts to
touch the stillness of the glass.

And as I watched a tiny boatman's oars
dipped perfectly across the surface,
pulling thousands of silk lines into
patterns of rippled light.

While above, dragonflies dived,
careering like First World War
fighter pilots from some pre-historic age,
plying their skills in capturing dinner
across the warm, sunny air.

Pond on Army Land – Hilary Gregory

and I am inside outside,

in a world too small to join

where tiny things push up coils of

earth and sparrows hop from

blade to blade and I

forget to breathe

as my dreams are kept prisoner

by the creatures that live on the

inside of Army land.

Hilary Gregory

Red Is Not Always For Danger

The Chelsea Pensioners in their bright red coats
Enter the hall with pride.
The robes of red worn by the choir
As they sing in harmony side by side.
The military red in the coloured flags,
The red on the side of the drum.
Red are the poppies worn in the hats
Of the men and the women whose fine work is done
In the wars where the blood and the flames are red
And the heroes are part of our times.
Red is hot anger felt by the masses
When terrorists get away with their crimes.
Now the November evening draws to a close
After a sunset so red in the sky,
And the prayers of the clergy reach out to the world
As the trumpets sound their goodbye.
Then the poppies so red flutter down from above
And the number of poppies is high
It's time to remember the flowers in the fields
Where the red poppies quiver and bend
To remember the fallen in wars then and now
With a hope to have peace in the end.

Peggie Keeley

Jam Jar

Christina Cummings

A ropey strand of seaweed grips and chills my bare feet. Dark bottle-green, with dimpled purple pods, it floats on a patch of seawater left by the tide. Further out, the white foam laps at the ever-moving feet of small children, collecting fluted shells in plastic buckets or cramming smooth round pebbles into much worn pockets in sandy shorts. Pastel grey gulls swoop over the shoreline, screeching like witches in their daily ritual to find food. And oystercatchers run in staccato, stopping suddenly to bend and prise open mussels and razor clams with their long strong bills.

Short bare trees high up on the cliffs' edge seem to be leaning, straining, in spiky fear, away from the pull of the sea, and out across the bay on the grassy headland, the stripey outline of the old lighthouse pierces the gloom with a tunnelling prick of light. A single beam traverses the slashed angles of ancient rocks. It moves quickly and then holds a yellow flickering spotlight - a moment here, and then moves out onto the near blackness that will soon enshroud the rolling ocean.

Jam Jar – Christina Cummings

My glass jar smells fishy and sour and strangely sweet and several minnows are resting on the bottom, their mouths stretching widely. I tip them back into the coolness of the rock pool and rinse out the jar. Nearby a group of laughing boys are trying to pry off the largest limpets and periwinkles with strong sticks, one of them drawing Jolly Rogers in the wet sand with his toes.

Then, all about me, a subtle shift of colour and light, the brassy glow on the faces of the last few people leaving the beach, the ochre-blueness of the stiff cliff side path. Evening's approach always surprises. I follow the others up the chalky path, my empty glass jar swinging by it's frayed loop of string. When we reach half way, where the path makes a sharp left turn, then rises again more steeply, I look back at the bay. As I turn my salt whipped cheeks to the east, the wind takes away my breath, and I have to take a gulp of air to breathe. From up here the rock pools appear small, like mere puddles, but further out, the flapping green waves roll into the bay and crash onto the shoreline, making criss-crossed patterns as they flatten and spread out like spilt drinks, then drain backwards again, as a shift in the tide lures them in once more to the vastness of the sea.

Total Solar Eclipse

For once in her life, she arrived on time
At the place where he'd asked her to be.
As he clasped her hand, pointed up at the sky,
A darkness crept in from the sea.

The shade of the Moon traced an arc on the Earth
As it pushed before the Sun's face.
The temperature dropped as totality struck,
The Corona blazed out into space.

As the Moon inched away, the Sun dazzled out
Like a diamond ring, she could see.
And the dawn rushing in from the West lit her face
When he asked, 'Will you marry me?'

Maria Watson

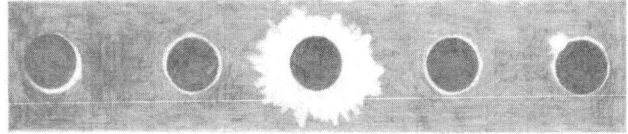

Flitting on a Friday at the Jubilee Clock Circa 1964
Carole Hastings

The lumbering lorry pulls up sharp, disgorging the factory girls for their Friday frenzy. I'm right where I'm told to be, by the Jubilee Clock. There's Mum in her usual position wedged between Lynette's chunky chest and Mrs English's thin lips. They tumble out empty-bagged but with pay-day-full purses except Mrs English of course. She swings into St Luke's seeking her weekly absolution for the bulging bags of bounty pilfered from the company canteen.

I'm swooped up in seconds deposited in Dewhurst watching an eagle eye inspection of New Zealand lamb shoulders. We dodge the traffic - me to Woolworth's for sugary shorties - mum to British Home Stores for cheese so processed that it polystyrenes your palette. We converge by the green grocer - King Edwards, cauli, cookers and cabbage - no other fruit - that comes in tins. Leap into Lyons for silver Swiss rolls before bouncing to Boots - for a packet of Lux - not Cadam for Madam - mustn't forget the Amami - it's hair night tonight.

We're rounding the bend now, me into International - Princes pilchards, pears and mandarins, large eggs and best bacon - not too much fat or it's going straight back. Mum veers to Victor Value for all the O's - Omo, Bisto, Paxo, Typhoo [oh an 'O' too many ...] plus two tins of Farrow's - that's where the best peas went you know, it's all topped up with Oxtail soup - Crosse and Blackwell if you don't mind - not that Heinz stuff - too watery by half.

We're on the final leg, a flit into Foxes for fags, fuel for the lighter and a bar of Cadbury's 3d just for me. Phew! A wend down Wendover Road and we're home. Key in door, gallop to kitchen, kettle on - job well done.

Memory

My memory is my life, my reason, it's me,
Without my memory who would I be?
Childhood days of pleasure and fun,
Teddy bears' picnics, swings in the sun,
Dressing up clothes, wearing mum's shoes,
Birthday parties, reading books to choose.
Wobbling on bikes, pushing wheels on a dog,
Ford Anglia cars, teddy boys, yellow smog.
Christmas fun, Easter and Whit walks,
Bonfire toffee, making stuffed Guy Fawkes.
Teachers, school friends to whom I still write a letter,
Doctors and nurses in hospital made me better.
Black Jacks, Fruit Salads, fizzy pop, hard to digest.
Drooling over Davy Jones and footballer George Best.
The Beatles, Rod Stewart, 10CC and Status Quo,
Out on the razz, Night Fever at the disco.
Buying my first mini and driving it home,
Getting a flat, living there on my own.
Classes and masses of children I knew,
Watching them bloom as their confidence grew.
Meeting the person that one day I'd marry,

Memory – Gill Johnson

Feeling the kick of the babies I carry.
Giving birth in a room so sterile and white,
Feeding, teething, through a long dark night.
Our children's first steps, going to school,
Football, dancing, the first length in the pool.
Savouring holidays in different places,
Ski-ing quite badly and losing the races.
Autumn mists rising in a Venice lagoon,
Warm nights in Tuscany, meals lit by the moon.
White sands and dolphins, silver fish in a net,
A cool glass of wine watching a Florida sunset.
Christmas in Munich, markets in the snow,
Watching and helping as my family grow.
Loved ones with us and loved ones past,
Knowing life's fleeting and does not last.
My memory is my life, my reason, it's me,
Without my memory who would I be?

Gill Johnson

Fish Wife

First, she wanted the stingray clutch bag
(Made with the skins of several unfortunate rays.)
I was stung for 2000 dollars
and she was hooked:
pulled out and reeled in.
She ordered the matching purse.

Next, it was pink Dior salmon-skin shoes.
Strong as crocodile they say, *yet soft*.
So soft, they also made a salmon skin bikini:
the Skini. They cast out mail-shots,
baited their lines with adverts in *Vogue*,
and waited, patiently, for her to bite.

Three can swim in this pool, I decided, when the *skini* arrived.
I peered into the depths of the world wide web
and spotted *oceanleather.com* flickering, just under the surface.
I ordered myself a catfish briefcase,
dropped the Barclaycard inside (splosh!)
and locked it.

Kirsty Whittle

For the Sake of a Few Dead Roses
Sonja Eagle

There it was again the scraping sound, metal on metal, a vague quiet scratching that sent loud bells ringing in my head, waking me from a fretful and unhelpful sleep. Icy fingers gripped my guts and squeezed hard, my breathing turned into short gasps and my mind, well my mind spun in a vortex of horror and fear. He was home, key in hand desperately trying to find the lock to insert it in.

I could hear my daughter snoring gently in her innocent sleep, in the bedroom behind me. Trusting me to keep her in a world of dolls and make-believe and fairies and gentle childhood things. She was starting to wonder, she was starting to be aware. I noticed her quizzical looks, her questions. Is Daddy in a bad mood again? Is Daddy sleeping this morning?

I looked around our rented furnished flat with its old heavy furniture, its big bay windows and high ceilings; it wasn't a haven, it wasn't safe, it wasn't home. God knows I worked hard enough to keep us all here, smart personal assistant by day to a University professor, bar work in the evening. Nobody knew, nobody could tell, I was always lively, funny and full of jokes. Couldn't let them know my dark secret, my shame, my awful other life. How could I ever explain the swirling drama that was my home life, the ever decreasing circles of played out emotional drama? The attacks physical and verbal, the tears afterwards mostly his not mine, the recriminations the apologies, the pleading, his not mine. His, 'Let's start again if you really love me.' And start again we did sometimes a few weeks in between sometimes just a few days but always the same outcome. My acceptance of whatever came to me and my blind faith that it would get better and that this time would be the last time. But once again I would accept a few dead roses, probably from the local park, and his sad anguished pleadings of need for his small family.

The key turned in the lock. I could hear him muttering to himself and singing softly, a tuneless song that could have been a lament. This was a bad sign if he came in really drunk he would just go to bed and fall asleep, but a good mood meant he would try and be friendly and chatty. This was worse as he would talk, mostly gibberish and then get frustrated when I didn't make the correct responses. However hard I tried I couldn't get it right. Then the anger would start, normally the verbal abuse would be first. I was stupid. I was a slut. Why didn't I understand his pain? This would continue until he worked himself up to the physical outlet for his frustration. Normally just a couple of slaps, then the punches, but he had grown clever over the years and took to holding my head by my hair and banging my head on the wall. The bruises don't show on your head. It embarrassed him when I had had to explain how I broke my finger or why I had walked into yet another cupboard and got a black eye. No, he was much cleverer by now, the damage went mostly unseen, the physical damage that is. My sense of worthlessness and isolation continued in a drip drip of abuse, the need for secrecy all-consuming for both of us.

It wasn't like this all the time sometimes there were good times, sometimes we could go out as the small family we were and have fun but you could never tell how the day would end.

Nine years of accepting his control and being crippled by fear and it snapped. No more. He started straight away with a whack round the head, what had I done to make the door so difficult to open? I stood in my pyjamas shaking and with an unknown strength picked up the old, very heavy bedside cabinet and threw it at him, he collapsed in a heap on the floor, sobbing don't hurt me please.

My journey from victim to survivor had started his from bully to coward.

April

Di Reid

T.S. Eliot said 'April is the cruellest month'. Well, that's his opinion and he's entitled to say what he likes. I am entitled to empower myself, to emphasise that April was a damn good month. How pretentious does that sound?

'Those April showers they come your way.'

But not to stay darling. Did you know that April has been designated Stress Awareness Month for the 19th year? Not many people know that. Who said that? But they do know about stress.

I am now trying desperately to be stressed for April. Listening to the news is a good start. The price of petrol, looking in the mirror first thing in the morning, standing on the scales. Was that pain indigestion or heart failure? How many more spare parts is my husband going to end up with? Why, as the daffodils herald the start of sunny days and blue skies, do I need to feel despondent? I could go on manufacturing stress, conjuring it up, deliberating, pretending. No, I have decided to come right out and say, April was a very good month. Not is, will be, but definitely was.

It was a good month remembered. It awakened the senses, falling in love for the first time. Walking hand in hand, dreaming, dreamy, heady, happy. Revelling in the never-ending glorious days of April. I was living in the moment, for the moment. It was good, so good. Would it ever end? At the time I thought please no, let it go on forever, but yes it did.

'Those were the days my friend, we thought they'd never end.'

Now I sit smiling in quiet moments to myself, still smiling after fifty years. Oh April you were the best month ever.

Diamond Finish
Madeleine Woosnam

Half an hour to go. She looked at her watch again. Ran her fingers over its smooth face, stroked it. The watch that *he* had given her, along with so many false promises. She sighed and gazed out of the window. It had been a slow day today. The recession had really hit the High Street. People just weren't coming in to try on anymore. Not even for a laugh at lunchtime.

Twenty minutes. Would the day never end? Cara looked at her freshly painted nails. Damn. One of them was chipped already. She surreptitiously slipped a pot of "Diamond Finish Precious Pink" from under the counter and repaired the damage. A diamond, that was all she wanted, in particular one on the fourth finger of her left hand.

Ten minutes. She pulled a hand mirror out of her bag and checked her make-up. Pouted as she applied another layer of "Raspberry Dream" to her already lipstick-laden lips. She knew she looked good. Barely nineteen and her skin and hair were perfect. Her figure immaculate and she didn't even have to exercise or watch what she ate. Her mother was always moaning on about how unfair it was that middle age was showing itself in her own thickening waist and thighs. Cara permitted a small smile to play about her lips admiring the way that a dimple danced on her left cheek and her eyes turned up at the corners.

'I don't know what you've got to smile about, young lady.' grumbled the voice of her supervisor, Claire. 'There'll be no commission for you this month with figures the way they are. You've not sold anything for days.'

Cara sighed. It was true. Sales had been dire and she desperately needed the commission to meet the mortgage payments on her flat. What was the point of being the mistress of a rich man if he didn't even provide for her? She smiled vaguely at Claire. Let her moan. Poor woman was past it at 41. She clearly had no life of her own.

Finally, six o'clock. Cara picked up her bag, flung her jacket over her shoulder, threw a hurried goodbye at Claire and was out of the shop before Claire could call her back to complete some unnecessary task.

As Cara hurried towards the tube station she allowed herself to think of Max. Married man with three children and a life of his own, and lover of Cara for the last thirteen months and twenty-five days. The "Uncle" Max of her childhood, her father's best friend from University, who had been on family holidays with them, laughed with her parents, built sandcastles with her and her brother, who had taught her to do a handstand at the age of six, played the piano as she danced. Held her hand when they went to see Jurassic Park and she was frightened.

Held her hand under the table on that Christmas Eve. Kissed her so tenderly under the mistletoe when no one else was around. And looked into her eyes as he stroked her face. And told her that he loved her.

Cara shivered, in spite of the warmth of the June evening, and hurried on. Tonight Max was all hers. They were going to the Ballet. Romeo and Juliet. Cara had been looking forward to it for weeks, ever since Max had produced the tickets as they lay intertwined in her small bed, the sun shining through the slatted blinds and striping their bodies so that it was hard to tell where his ended and hers began. Sometimes they went to his house and made love in his bed. The one he shared with his wife. And Cara couldn't help feeling a small sense of power that she was truly taking her place, until it was time to leave and she would look sadly round the room and touch Meg's things as if realising their permanence in the face of her ... what? And as Max withdrew both physically and emotionally and as she left the house alone, the guilt would flood in and she would vow never to meet him again. Until the next time.

'I promise I'll leave her by Christmas. Be patient sweetheart.' Or 'I can't upset the applecart at the moment. Louisa has her GCSE's.' Or 'We'll go away together, just you and me. Somewhere warm. You'd like that wouldn't you? Just as soon as Meg has got her mother settled in the home.' And so on. Promises that fell unchecked from his lips. Promises that he knew she wanted to hear. Promises that she still believed, like a fool. But tonight Cara refused to be daunted or upset. Tonight was hers. His and hers, and it was going to be such a beautiful night. She had wanted to be a ballerina as a child. Had pored endlessly over books of Margot Fonteyn and Darcey Bussell. Had imagined herself feted and adored, gorgeous in her costumes.

Cara hurried up the steps at the Royal Opera House. Just time for a quick check in the ladies and then she would meet him in the bar as planned. She hummed to herself as she fluffed up her hair and smoothed down her dress from the shop's new collection. It fitted her perfectly and hinted at sophistication beyond her years, very different from the sort of outfits she wore to go clubbing with her friends. It had cost her a lot, even with the discount. But it was worth it. It was important to look her best for him and she knew she did.

She made her way into the bar. Settled herself on a barstool, smiled at the barman and ordered a Bacardi and coke. Glanced up as a familiar figure made it's way towards her. And froze as her father's voice said. 'There'll be no ballet for you tonight. I think you'd better come home with me.'

Doing the Right Thing
Carole Hastings

'Well Dad, what do you think?' Stephen's question is surplus to requirements. Giles puts his arm around his son's shoulder and steers him through the French doors onto the terrace. Stephen was his first-born - his pride and joy.

'What do I think? I think it's wonderful as long as you're sure it's really for you. How long has your mother had the inkling? She's done well to keep it from me.' The late evening sun bathes the terrace and rose garden in a golden hue mirroring the moment. They stroll through the walled garden, fruit espaliers groaning with the season's bounty, to the summerhouse, Giles' sanctuary overlooking the lake.

'Ran it by Ma a few weeks ago. She always used to talk about going to watch the State Opening of Parliament and life in the public eye being the daughter of an MP, so I thought I'd sound her out first. Gramps died when I was so young I felt I needed to talk to her to get an inside track.' Stephen sips his scotch and soda, eying his father's reaction.

'And what did she have to say?' Giles settles himself into his Sultan's chair - the rattan creaking and stretching around his frame. His jaw twitches fighting to suppress the grin his muscles would prefer to make.

'Well, she said to do my best to keep the twins out of the public eye wherever I could - that's certainly not the party line though. They love the package: local lawyer with mixed race human rights lawyer for a wife and two beautiful bright kids at state schools. Ma also made a song and dance about sticking on the straight and narrow and the importance in not having any skeletons on the closet. The local party chairman's already clobbered me on that one, such is the power of the press, so they both agree on that at least - albeit they vote for different parties. I should get the nod tomorrow - just wanted to talk to you first. Pretty safe seat and not too far from here. Rachel's thrilled - after all, she was the activist at uni - not me. If it wasn't for the twins it would be her throwing her hat into the ring not me.'

'I'm sure she would.' Giles grins with more than a little devilment. 'Gramps would have had a fit - his grandson standing as an MP for the other side. That said, he'd respect you for sticking to your beliefs. If you do get in son, two things. Just make sure you don't ban shooting and that I'm not taxed to within an inch of my life. I've worked damned hard for this place, and to keep your mother in the custom to which she feels entitled. She'd have the screaming ab-dabs if we had to sell up. Such is her influence in the world of horticulture she's now planning on getting her garden on the National Gardens Scheme - probably because it would be the biggest in the area ... '

Father and son share a flash of mischief that evaporates as Faith appears, predictable in pumps, pearls and pashmina.

'The twins are getting tired darling and Rachel thinks they ought to be in bed soon - much as we don't want you to go it might make sense as they're pretty fractious'. Faith takes the empty glasses from her husband and son and directs her hard gaze at Giles.

'Well Pa, what do you make of your son's impending news? Rather something that you might have liked to do if you hadn't been so busy in the City.' The lunge was unexpected as the dodge.

'Couldn't have afforded the manor to which you thought you should have been born if I had and that would never have done my dear.' Faith knows better than to start a spat and marches off with knitted brows and downturned mouth towards their house.

'So, some things don't change then Dad?' Stephen had sat through too many sniper attacks to recount.

'It's pathological with your mother Stephen - I gave up trying to please her years ago - she's got her pile and I've got my sailing, shooting and business interests - and I'm pretty immune to most of her nonsense to be honest.'

'Why have you stayed after all these years? And did you really want to be an MP? We've never talked about it - I just knew you always encouraged me.'

'Gramps opened all the doors I needed for business - I had no old school tie after all. Leave? Life's rarely a bed of roses and we have our good days. As for politics, well I gave it some thought at one time but no, not really. I loved the cut and thrust of business and all it could bring. I'm too greedy to be an MP son. I enjoy the good life.'

'So you don't think you can have both Dad?' Stephen's Porsche Cayenne is parked on the gravel drive where Rachel straps the twins into the back seat. Giles shakes his head, leans in and kisses them both.

'You know you have to be extra well behaved now that Daddy's going to be an MP.' Giles catches Faith's raised eyebrow and stands watching the car until the taillights resemble glowworms darting from sight. The voice behind him cuts into the balmy night,

'The twins are not the only ones who need to be very well-behaved now and I really hope for Stephen's sake, you've covered your tracks Giles.' Faith waits for no response and Giles returns to the summerhouse via the scotch bottle where he lingers as the purples and reds of the sky become black.

*

'When are you going to give me the bad news Giles?' The words seep out in a whisper as Verity rolls onto her side. Her erstwhile soul-mate's long-faced anguish needs little interpretation. It has been reinforced with perfunctory lovemaking and swift dressing.

'Is it really that obvious?' Giles takes a pack of cigarettes from his pocket, lights one and goes up on deck, away from the cocoon of the cabin below. Seagulls swoop in the blindingly bright sky and the sun paints shadows on the foredeck. He slumps into the cockpit, head bowed, elbows on knees. He draws hard, coughs and stares down the companionway at Verity calmly dragging on her clothes and shaking her dishevelled hair. He's never envisaged this day and unlike most things in his life, is ill-prepared for an act he does not want to make. In three strides she's by his side, taking the cigarette from his lips and hurling it into the sea. Together they watch it float towards the horizon.

'It's a helluva while since you've had one of those damn things. Come on, I'm sure you've done worse in your time than tell me it's over. Just speak to me.' Her calm voice is betrayed by the hurt in her eyes, the beautiful expressive violet eyes that flash when they meet his in laughter and lovemaking.

'I feel a total shit Verity.'

'I'm sure I'll agree, but at least tell me why. I thought we were soul-mates, Giles, real soul-mates. We're not just a middle-aged couple who betray their spouses every Friday to relieve the bloody boredom. I can't believe that I haven't picked up any vibe before. But I know where this is going, I just don't know why ... '

'There's not been a vibe to pick up. I really really love you. Being with you makes me so utterly happy but I'm sorry I've got to end it, now.' Giles' voice trails off as Verity looks at him, almost into him. 'I, I have to ... '

'Why now? I've never put you under any pressure for more than we have. We've joked enough about "why have the moon when we've got the stars" stuff. I thought this relationship worked for both of us?' She holds up a hand to stop him from interrupting.

'You already think Faith suspects you're seeing someone and you know she doesn't really mind as long as you fund her and it doesn't interfere with her bridge afternoons or relentless gardening.' Verity looks down at the wedding band and shakes her head.

'I pretty sure that Ralph knows I'm playing away. But he doesn't give a damn, as long as I attend the ladies evenings at the Lodge and host his interminable business dinners, charming potential clients - playing the game. We serve their purposes and I thought we served each other's, as lovers and kindred spirits.' Verity hugged her knees to her chest and waited for a response.

'It's not Faith or Ralph I'm thinking of. It's my son Stephen. He wants to be an MP. His local candidate's not going to stand next time and he's in the frame, but has been told "no skeletons". They can't afford a scandal. They got too much mileage out of the Oaten affair. The press are sniffing round and I can't let him down. I just couldn't bear to wreck his chances with some "Lawyer's Father in Sex Scandal Shock" headline.' Giles reaches out to Verity, but she slides to the other side of the cockpit.

'Stephen an MP? I don't even think he's particularly bright. They'll make mincemeat of him in the House. You're the orator in your family; you're the one with the political convictions, you're the one that's nudged him all the way so he achieves what you'd really like for yourself.'

The arrow's not wide off its mark and Giles knows there little point of a rejoinder. He sits in silence fiddling with the winch while Verity ends her tearful tirade.

'So I'm being cast aside for the sake of his political career, although there's no proof anyone knows anything about us. Not loving me would be bad enough, but this is just a joke.' Escaping Giles' grasp Verity starts the engine. Giles hauls up the anchor for the last time and in silence as heavy as the blackening sky, they motor back to Lymington marina. Nearing Giles' berth, their final charade is complete: Verity dives below whilst Giles brings the boat in on his own and leaps off with the mooring lines. He secures her with a flourish and turns off the engine.

Verity then emerges, eye make-up and lips bold and beautiful. Walking along the pontoon with head held high and without looking back, she slips into her Mini Cooper by the gate. But today, no blast of The Eagles or Steppenwolf, just the sound of her own weeping accompanies her on the drive back home.

Giles' footsteps to the car park are slow with sadness. He throws away the empty Chablis bottle, avoiding the gaze of any fellow sailors. For the first time in his life he's put his own desires second. Well and truly second. He can't quite believe it. Verity makes him happier than he can remember, but Stephen needs a clean family bill of health to make it to Government. To be in Government is the whole purpose of a politician. Such a sacrifice has to be made. He would do it for himself. He would do it for his son. For his wife? No. No, he would never give up Verity for her. As he gets into his Lexus he looks at his phone - two missed calls from Faith. He'll be home soon enough ...

He pulls up at his house to find Stephen's car parked by the steps for the second time this week. The patchwork quilt of colours, the heavenly scents of lavender and honeysuckle and the gentle buzz of nectar loving bees, calm his anxiety as he strides to the open front door. Faith's red-rimmed eyes dart at him as he enters the sitting room and Stephen, face pale and pinched, leaps to his feet. Giles leans to hug him, their limbs barely touch.

'Hello Dad. I've got some bad news to tell you. It'll be in the press tomorrow - I had to come to see you and Ma first.'

'Sit down and tell me what it is, I can see your mother's upset. Can it be all that bad Stephen?'

Sheepishly Stephen shuffles onto the chintz-covered chair opposite his parents.

'It is, and it's well and truly scuppered my political career I'm afraid. I've been a bit cavalier with some business deals. Wanting it all I guess ... The Sun have found out I've had money from property developers to oil some wheels. They're hanging me out to dry. I'm so sorry to do this to you and Ma. I haven't even told Rachel yet.' Giles drops onto the sofa next to his wife. A large grainy photo on Faith's lap shows Stephen with a barely-clad blonde, their heads bent over a coffee table, hovering above some lines of fine white powder.

'Yeah that too I'm afraid Dad. A wild party with the developers. Just a crazy time that ... '

Giles cuts in, his voice hoarse,

'It's not just your political career that's over Stephen, you bloody idiot. You'll not have many clients come knocking at your door when this gets out. I doubt Rachel will stick around either. And who can blame her? How much? How much did you make?'

Head in hands, Stephen's words falter, 'A million. But they haven't paid it all yet.'

Giles shakes his head in utter disbelief, 'I bet they haven't. And now they won't need to, son.'

Giles gets to his feet, goes into his study and gently closes the door. He flicks on the Bose, his finger pulsing until the music drowns out the screaming in his head. How could his son be so stupid? His phone bleeps. A voicemail from Verity. He pictures her: wild hair trailing in the breeze, her smile fading from her lips. Call Back or Delete? He taps the latter. His world - changed, smaller and sullied is no place for his soul-mate now. He wants to laugh at the absurdity of the situation, but instead he softly weeps.

Peacock Street

Christina Cummings

He lives with one constant; his apartment feels perpetually cold. North facing. The shattered back of night has somehow broken, and it's now morning. The early sun strains to shine through thickly lined incontinent clouds. It sifts through the gnarly plane trees and rakes the gravel of the community basketball court as it ascends into the greyness. Smearing the department store windows it bounces off the pigeons that roost on the moss-covered tiles and then it does a leap right over Peacock Street.

The potted basil and lemon grass he's placed beside the sink droop, like despondency, over the ledge of the tiled windowsill, where Mifty sits staring out at the birdbath. A blue-smoke Persian cat with half a tail, Mifty never leaves the flat. The other half of her tail having lodged itself in the unforgiving slam of a car door means the closest she gets to fresh air these days is sitting just behind the wavering cat-flap, with a teasing closeness.

The phone rings. Shrill insistence that cannot be ignored. Mifty shifts from hind legs to forelegs and back again. Raoul raises his head from the sofa, then grabs a shaggy cushion and clamps it to his ear. The answer-phone machine clicks in and a woman's voice screams 'Wake up, I know you're there!' The line crackles, a far-away rainstorm sort of hiss. 'Damn you Raoul!' she says. And there's a silence then, followed by a sharp sound; a book falling from a shelf perhaps, or a sharp sob.

Later, Raoul would delete the message without listening to it. But for now, he sleeps off the disappointment, and the vodka, his arm dangling to the floor like a broken rudder.

*

Annalise frames the view with her hands, she looks past the sculptural hedgerows and the wrought iron gates, to the three storey apartment block, where behind Venetian blinds, the modern aluminium kind, her lover lies sleeping in his basement flat. She knows he's in there. His bike leans against the wall, the lock securely fastened to a rusted padlock chain. He never goes anywhere without his bike. And there's something else; Mifty looks relaxed, as only she is when he is there.

A bin lorry pulls up across the street, obscuring her view, like a slow stage curtain. Pulling her coat around her, she moves on down Peacock Street. She passes a hotdog vendor, hesitates for a moment, decides the clawing feeling in her stomach isn't hunger, then walks eastwards past the Lucky House restaurant, where Raoul had once proposed to her, wrapping a jumbo shrimp around her middle finger, then stopping several times on the way home, leaning against the peeling bus stop and the old red phone box, their arms entwined.

She remembered as clear as light the morning after, what he in his darkness, forgot. And she was not going to stop until she'd reminded him.

Over the Garden Wall
Di Reid

Lettie was busy attacking the weeds in her garden. Her grey hair tied severely back and her sturdy body bending to the task in hand. She was into third world techniques, and slash and burn came to mind as she pruned viciously, scattered weed killer everywhere, killing slugs, snails and aphids and not quite the neighbours cat Henry, as he jumped with some agility out of the way of Lettie's well aimed garden hose.

She heard voices next door, and climbed onto the ledge to look over the wall to see Gilly Hawkins coming up the path with a friend. She was just about to make herself known and complain about the wretched cat, when she heard her name mentioned. Crouching down behind the wall, and feeling slightly ridiculous she was aware of footsteps approaching, and voices becoming louder.

Now dear reader, what was it that Lettie Jennings will hear to make her fall off the ledge into the rose bushes, emerge confused, scratched, dirty, trip over the bloody cat, fall in and out of the wheel barrow, bang her head on the path, and stagger into the kitchen?

She actually made it to a chair and put her head in her hands. What was Gilly saying in a loud voice, thought Lettie?

'We all know Henry likes a bit of the other.'

Henry was the cat. No, she said Harry, Lettie's husband.

'I saw him with his arm around that young bloke in the "Kings Arms". He's the talk of the village.' Lettie promptly passed out. Gilly and her friend also collapsed into chairs, laughing and giggling.

'That'll teach the nosey old bat, always hiding behind the wall listening to conversations that are none of her business.' They were breathless, sides heaving with hysterical laughter.

Lettie was breathless too when Harry found her on the kitchen floor. What the hell had happened? Blood everywhere. He phoned for an ambulance, but didn't give much hope for the poor old girl.

In the depths of her unconscious being, Lettie Jennings felt a stirring. She had been in a fearsome fight with an unknown enemy in the undergrowth. Bruised and battered she may be, but there were three reasons to rise again and do battle. Gilly, Harry and that bloody cat Henry. Vengeance is not the prerogative of the Lord, it's mine.

Suffrage

Banners held high
For all to see
Please, oh please, look at me

I'm a Woman I'm a Woman
Not a slave
Even prepared to dig a grave

The rich, the poor
The destitute
Women of every kind of suit

History tells us how it was
Hear their cries
Hear their sobs

The women of a by-gone age
Who fought so hard to pave the way
For better times for you and me

"Votes for Women" it has to be

Marjorie Andrews

Book 501

Maria Watson

My Dad was a printer. My grandparents arranged for him to leave school as he turned fifteen, to take up an apprenticeship at "The East Kent Times". There he learned to use lead type, black ink and newsprint to create the local paper. They had "given him a trade" and for the next fifty years, he had ink permanently ingrained beneath his fingernails as he earned his living and kept his family. He also nursed the reverence for literature that only an academically inclined man, thwarted by circumstance, could have.

In the 1970s, Dad landed his dream job in the printing department of the Cambridge University Library. Mostly he printed exam papers, but occasionally he printed books. There was an export ban with China, and professors either side of the Bamboo Curtain circumvented it by swapping facsimiles of their precious documents. One day Dad came home bubbling with excitement. He had been given the unpublished first version of "Isaac Newton's Cambridge Lectures on Optics" to turn into a limited edition. Handwritten in Latin by the great man, Dad carefully photographed each page, turned it into a printing plate, and printed it in brown ink on thick, cream paper. He folded, gathered and sewed the pages together, added the endpapers, then trimmed them square with a guillotine. Finally he sent them to the bindery to be glued into a brown case with the title blocked on the spine in gold letters. Five hundred of these beautiful books were duly shipped to the Far East and the University Library received facsimiles of Charles Darwin's lecture notes in return.

Book 501 was an extra copy made by Dad to smuggle home and share with his family. When he handed it to me, I reluctantly put down my "Jackie" magazine and flicked through the pages of unintelligible writing. Then something caught my eye: Newton had sketched a prism with a beam of white light entering one side, splitting up into a rainbow before it exited the other. He must have jotted this down just after he did his famous experiment for the very first time, centuries before Pink Floyd adopted it for their album cover and my physics teacher chalked it up on the blackboard. So this was what scientific research was about: someone imagining a truth about the world in which we live, devising an experiment to test the idea, rigging up the apparatus and then carefully recording what they saw. I decided right then that I wanted to be a research scientist like Isaac Newton.

Dad gave me the book when I left home to read Natural Sciences at University. When I graduated, he presented me with an antiquarian book of lectures on astronomy to go with it. Then, a few years later, as he proudly watched me slide my PhD thesis between them on the bookshelf, he said,

'Well done. I think you may be the first person in our family to write a book, instead of print it.'

The Moon and Our Stars

The moon hangs heavy in the sky
dark shadows silently creeping by
its grey and silky surface
softly, gently, weeping

The waning moon, its cold pale face,
my heart with heavy longing
for loves lost lust still lingers deep
within my memories not asleep

And then the moon lets go its hold
as my upward gaze is dazzled,
a bright and vibrant light beams forth
to pierce the darkened shadows

At once I feel the warmth, your glow,
softening, comforting and with one swift blow
rekindling the love we had so strong
to stay with me the whole night long

The Moon and Our Stars – Sally Thompson

It never will seem fair to me
but, in my moments of despair, I see
You are up there still, my love,
shining brightly from above.

And all around you are the rest,
a galaxy, a trillion stars; the best.
All heroes, and, just like you,
stand guarding, watching, all we do.

For it was not just then you kept us safe
but still you mind us from your heavenly place
And so, my love, my hearts delight, I see you, always,
strong and bright, forever warming the moonlit night.

Sally Thompson

Snow on Christmas Morning

Unwrapping the snowstorm carefully:
turning it giddily on its axis,
we watched the falling snow
submerge the town.

Last night the world had turned,
as a million fairies tossed
their jewels into the air
to fly and dance in cold mists,
re-sculpting trees, houses and walls
into a flower garden of possibilities
beneath soft, white-lace, sheets.

 After the whirling winds of the storm
the scattered sky, lay in blankets
over the restlessness, settling
us softly, sleepily, silently.

Until waking up on Christmas
morning, we heard a voice inside
us calling: 'Go, and make your
earthling tracks
in the pristine snow.'

Snow on Christmas Morning – Hilary Gregory

Putting the snowstorm gently
down, we went outside to find
that the snow-globe was our town
and we were adrift under millions
of hexagonal jewels of water and light,
with the soft white calling
and the light snow falling
as it had in the wild night.

Hilary Gregory

Joshua Frederick Arthur Scott Green

Joshua Frederick Arthur Scott Green.
You're there by the photo-er-copy machine,
chewing your biro and drinking your tea
and noticing everyone here, except me.

Joshua Frederick Arthur Scott Green.
I know where you're going, I know where you've been.
I saw your CV –yes, I looked a quick sneak
when I was in HR on Tuesday last week.

Joshua Frederick Arthur Scott Green.
You went to the poly at Walton-on-Nene,
got a 2:2 grade in media studies
and base-jumped for Children In Need with your buddies.

Joshua Frederick Arthur Scott Green.
You speak to that girl from accounts called Charlene:
you straighten your tie, put your foot on her chair
And you smile at her jokes while she plays with her hair.

Joshua Frederick Arthur Scott Green.
The lads come in buzzed up on instant caffeine:
they drag you to lunch for a steak and a beer
while I unwrap my egg and cress sandwich right here.

Joshua Frederick Arthur Scott Green.
I look at you now and I sigh and I dream
of a future before us, of marriage and kids
and lots of small Joshuas sat in their bibs.

For *I* can tell jokes, *I* can twiddle my hair,
I could base jump (I think) and I'm sure I've a flair
for eating a steak and for drinking a beer.
Oh Joshua – when will you see that I'm here?

Joshua Frederick Arthur Scott Green.
I sit with my chin on my hands and I seem
to wish every day away hoping a gleam
for laughter and loving with Joshua Green.

Kirsty Whittle

A Fairly Story
Gill Johnson

Long ago and far, far away, in a land wreathed in the mists of time called Plagiarism, lived a beautiful maiden called Slenderella. She lived with her chronologically gifted father and her two cosmetically challenged sisters, one of whom was exceedingly horizontally challenged and one who was very horizontally gifted. Her sisters who had non-discretionary fragrance from avoiding bathing were motivationally deficient and uniquely coordinated so they made Slenderella the domestic engineer in the house. Poor Slenderella had to dust the computers, make sure the waste disposal was not jammed, clean out the microwave and ensure their vast American fridge was full.

One day a bleep came from the security entry videophone and gazing at the screen the CCTV cameras showed that the mail delivery technician had come to the door with a next day highly priced special delivery that needed signing for or else it would be taken back to the depot. Having signed the plastic PDA Slenderella brought in an envelope which was grabbed by Chardonnay, the dry, fruity sister who ripped open the envelope and found it was a text invitation 'frm Pce

Plsng 4 a ball'. The other sister, Shiraz, the red, spicy one was overwhelmed to get such an invitation from Prince Pleasing as he was a Brad Pitt good looker and she yearned to meet him. Slenderella was pleased too, until those cruel sisters saw her pleasure and their hearts filled with malice and bad intent, even after having been on the Jeremy Vyle show and talking to the producers and the psychologists. They told Slenderella that SHE would not be going.

Slenderella was so upset that she ran out of the house and away into the dark deep forest where the day became night and the leaves were as thick as thieves. She began to feel scared as the light grew into gloom and a blank blackness settled all around. Suddenly just up ahead she spied a compact and bijou dwelling in need of some renovation with room for a garage. She knocked on the door and when no-one answered she pushed the door open and crept in. The large room looked like a student's bedroom at 1 o'clock on a Sunday afternoon. There was not a spare bit of floor to be seen. So armed with the Dyson she pulled out of a nearby cupboard, a bottle of Cillit Bang she found on the mantelpiece, a couple of cute squirrels, a badger, six bluebirds and a skunk that must have come from the zoo, she started a spring clean. *With a song in her heart she began to polish and dust, she and the animals worked fit to bust.*

After a short time the whole house was dazzling clean and the windows sparkled in the setting sun. Slenderella, the domestic goddess was just putting two more bay leaves in the boeuf bourguignon when the happy singing of seven vertically challenged people made her run to the window. At first these quaint characters thought that Slenderella was morally challenged, breaking into their house, but when they saw how clean and tidy their dwelling was and smelled the persuasive odours of her delicious cooking they realized her sweet nature and welcomed her to stay in their pad. When they heard about Slenderella's life at home they asked her to stay, but warned her not to wander too far in the forest as she would get lost.

The next day when Slenderella was in the house she decided to go for a walk. Not wanting to lose her way, she took with her some wheat free bread that she dropped at intervals so that she could find her way back to the cosy house and her new friends. After enjoying her quiet perambulation with her friends of the forest, the deer, the merry bluebirds and the frolicking rabbits, she turned to follow the trail back. To her horror she could not find the pieces of bread as they had been eaten by the merry bluebirds thinking she was feeding them. As no one had a Sat Nav they were all lost.

Wandering through the undergrowth for hours, they came upon a nasally gifted man who offered to show her the way to the edge of the wood and to buy her gold gloves for three beans. Slenderella was not bothered about the beans, but wanted to be shown the way, so she agreed. However once out of the wood she threw the beans away and settled down to rest while she pondered on what to do next. Tired Slenderella fell into a deep sleep and awaking next morning she found her world had turned into a green eyrie. Rubbing her eyes she realised that she was resting under an enormous beanstalk that must have grown magically from the beans she threw away. Looking up, the beanstalk curled and bent its way into the sky. Wondering where it reached Slenderella decided to climb it. However as most girls do when they are climbing trees, she became stuck and had to shout for help. A Deputy Prime Minister came by and seeing her plight asked her to let down her hair, so that he might come and join her. However his labour was not wanted by the liberal girl and she and the merry bluebirds decided democratically not to agree to this. So off he went into the forest, which is another Tory.

Eventually Slenderella realised that if she did not try to get down herself she would be on the beanstalk forever. She tried to climb down and managed, with great determination, to climb down by herself, as most girls do. But when she got down because she had touched the magical leaves and fronds, she fell into a deep sleep which made the merry bluebirds twitter with anxiety as no one could wake her.

Along came Three Little Pigs but try as hard as they might they could not wake her.

Along came Three Billy Goats Gruff but try as hard as they might they could not wake her.

Along came three bears but try as hard as they might they could not wake her.

Then along came a little girl in a scarlet hoodie and using unusual first aid techniques she had been taught at a scandalous school, she managed to wake Slenderella up by whispering that she had some CrazyFrog ring tones on her mobile which she would play. A bewildered Slenderella rubbed her eyes and Little Red, for that was the name of the hoodie wearing girl, took her to rest at her Grandmother's house. They knocked on the door and when Granny told them to lift the latch to open the door they walked in to see Granny having tea with a cross dressing wolf. This frightened Slenderella so much that she ran out of the door and ran. She ran, ran as fast as she could, down the path. Past a gingerbread man, past a woman, past a boy, past a girl, past a cow, past a horse, past a cat and past a dog to a field where a farmer was trying to pull up a very enormous turnip. Not wanting to stop, Slenderella shouted that there may be help coming and ran on.

Soon Slenderella reached a walled city and entering through the huge wooden gates, she was surprised to see the townsfolk all in the streets, talking about their Prince who was so unhappy that his unhappy thoughts were turning all the milk sour. Slenderella who was lactose intolerant was not too concerned about this, but not liking to see so many miserable human beings, walked up to the castle and demanded to see the Prince. A domestic luminary led her into the great golden throne room and when the Prince saw her, he began to smile and then to laugh. Poor Slenderella was bewildered by this, but when a large mirror was put in front of her Slenderella realised why he was laughing. Her hair was full of leaves, she had huge bean pods sticking to her clothes, there were several cobwebs lacing her skirt and a gingerbread man was sitting on her shoulder while six merry bluebirds flew around her head. As Slenderella had made him laugh for the first time in his life and she was not like any girl he knew, the prince asked her to marry him and to attend the ball he was holding at the weekend as his wife.

So Prince Pleasing had a new wife when he danced at the ball on Saturday; who wore a gown of gold woven by the famous designer Rumplestiltskin; who surprised her chronologically gifted father and her two cosmetically challenged sisters by being there; who appeared in the next edition of "Hiya" magazine and who, of course, lived happily ever after.

Biographies

Angela enjoys singing with her Whitchurch choir. When she isn't looking after her grandchildren or writing, she 'enjoys' being dragged daily for miles across fields by Swift, her lively border collie puppy.

Anne was born to travel. From her birth in Pakistan she has lived in many countries, appreciating the diverse cultures, languages and cuisine. Writing is an outlet for memories, family history and recipes from her past. Her computer keyboard still clicks.

Carole's passion for people-watching and travel put her on the long list for the Bradt/IOS Travel Writer of the Year 2011. Her first play was performed at the Chesil Theatre and a cookery book bubbles on her stove.

Chester-born Christina sang and taught her way around the world. Now living in Winchester, she is the mother of two amazing children who, despite their years, still listen to her stories. She is currently writing a novel.

Biographies

Claudia has been a doctor, florist and is a psychotherapist in training. She draws on her chaotic life as a divorced mother of four to write hilarious observation pieces.

Di was a nurse and has lived in Kuwait. Now in Lymington with her husband, she looks after her grandsons, enjoys bell ringing, piano and writing classes. She is a Cruse Bereavement Counsellor. Di watches weeds grow while creating stories.

Gill lives near Winchester and loves writing for fun and making up silly poems for her family. She enjoys champagne, watching sunsets and avoiding housework.

Hilary has settled in Winchester, after travelling the world. She has an immaculately kept house, is the adored mother of two perfectly behaved teenagers and is a successful writer and artist. All of her writing is fiction.

Jenny is a retired psychologist, which comes in handy as she loves writing about thoughts and feelings ... and the laptop never needs counselling. She plays bridge badly, and spends some time battling with her garden. She lives near Winchester with her husband.

Biographies

Kirsty squeezes as much writing as she can in between working as a Pilates teacher and being the mother of two teenage boys. She won two first prizes at the Winchester Writer's Conference 2011.

Madeleine enjoys writing, and performing in, the Easton pantomime. She also plays tennis and sings. Occasionally she remembers her husband, three children and dog whom she considers to be her major hobbies and ... she expects them to laugh at her jokes.

Marjorie has been married for 50 years and is the grandmother of two fine boys. She has a passion for learning especially about social history, gaining a BSc at 70. Her hobbies are water-colour painting, writing and stained glass.

As a child, Maria lost herself in historical fiction and constructed 'Blue Peter' models. Now, as an aerospace project manager and mother of three, she is writing a family history, whilst dreaming of impossible schedules and budgets.

Biographies

Peggie was born in Portsmouth in 1929, moving to Sussex in September 1939. She now lives near Winchester. Her interests are theatre, writing, reading and music. She is married with three grown up daughters, six grandchildren and two great grandsons.

Sally gave up hectic corporate life and commuting for the joy of having time to do some writing with a great group of women in Winchester. She also sews, reads, dreams and is a born again 'ski bum' in the French alps.

Sonja has retired from working in company management. She spends her new-found free time travelling and exploring new hobbies including jewellery-making and writing. She has two grown up children and lives in Winchester with her husband.